CRYSTAL CRAWLED UNDER THE PROPPED-UP WALL toward the safe. The space was much tighter than she had imagined. Then it dawned on her. *The wall is sinking back down!*

She hurried to get out, but as she did, she heard the wall shift. It brushed against her back as she pulled her head and shoulders free. Then the weight of the wall pushed her legs into the mud.

She tried to shove with her arms, but she was stuck tight.

Crystal panicked.

CRYSTAL'S MILL TOWN MYSTERY

STEPHEN AND JANET BLY

Chariot Books
DAVID C. COOK PUBLISHING CO.

A Quick Fox Book

Published by Chariot Books,
an imprint of David C. Cook Publishing Co.

David C. Cook Publishing Co., Elgin, Illinois 60120
David C. Cook Publishing Co., Weston, Ontario

CRYSTAL'S MILL TOWN MYSTERY

Cover illustration by Paul Turnbaugh
Cover and book design by Chris Patchel

First Printing, 1986
Printed in the United States of America
90 89 88 87 86   1 2 3 4 5

Library of Congress Cataloging-in-Publication Data

Bly, Stephen A.
  Crystal's mill town mystery.

  (A Quick fox book)
  Summary: Crystal and her friends discover a locked safe
in a burned-out lumber mill and find that they are not the
only ones interested in its contents.
  [1. Mystery and detective stories. 2. Idaho—Fiction] I. Bly,
Janet. II. Title.
PZ7.B6275Cp 1986   [Fic]   86-11591
ISBN 1-55513-054-2

For the real Gabrielle,
. . . hang in there, kid

CONTENTS

THE GLORY DAYS OF WINCHESTER MILL

I WONDER, WHAT'S THE DIFFERENCE BETWEEN A routine and a rut?" Crystal Blake threw the saddle across the back of her tall Appaloosa gelding, Caleb, and reached under him to grab the cinch.

"I suppose," she continued mumbling to herself, "it depends on whether you like what you are doing or not."

She smiled to herself, walked Caleb to the gate, closed it behind them, and headed toward the house. For over two months she had followed the same daily schedule. Ever since she and her family had moved from Southern California to the little mountain town of Winchester, Idaho, Crystal had gotten up at 6:00 in the morning to go out and take care of Caleb.

Every morning.

Rain, shine, wind, cold, heat (though in Winchester it never really got what Crystal called hot), and even now in the snow.

Every morning.

Then, every afternoon it was time to ride. Ride around town. Ride out in the Indian pasture with Gabrielle. Go over to Teresa Patterson's indoor arena with the high school rodeo team, or ride out across the prairie with Shawn Sorensen.

Every day it was the same.

And, every day, she absolutely loved it.

She left Caleb by the front of their wooden deck sidewalk and went into the house. Crystal's little sister, Allyson, had the living room couch covered with dolls. She heard her older sister, Karla, in a discussion with their mother upstairs in the tri-level home.

"Mother, I can't wear the yellow. You know that doesn't look good on me unless I have a good tan, and there is no way anyone here can have a good tan without a tanning lamp."

"Tanning lamps are dangerous, aren't they?" Catherine Blake answered her daughter as she sorted through some clothes in the closet.

Crystal stood at the door watching them. "Hey, you can wear one of my new western blouses," she suggested, half kidding, since she knew Karla had no interest in western clothes.

"The green one . . . the silky-looking green one with the lace?" Karla sounded serious.

"Yeah, sure . . ." Crystal stammered. "Are you kidding me?"

"No, I'm desperate." Karla turned and looked at Crystal. "Do you think it will fit me?"

"Well, it's only made for freshmen," Crystal giggled, "but I suppose you could survive for a few hours."

"Thanks, Crys . . . don't bother . . . I'll go down

to your room and get it." Karla raced down the stairs.

Mrs. Blake sighed. "If I can get Karla dressed every day, I think I've got it made. She did want something special tonight."

"Another Friday-night date with Michael?" Crystal asked.

"Not just any date, tonight she's going to The Ponderosa with Michael and his parents, Mr. and Mrs. Flannery."

"Wow! Bringing her home to momma! This is serious." Crystal laughed. "Mom, I'm going riding. Shawn and I are going to ride around the lake. If we have time we'll be running some practice rounds over in the pasture."

"Are you dressed warm enough? It's cold today. Listen, why don't you two ride by Norton's and bring home that meat I have waiting." Mrs. Blake walked with Crystal back down to the living room.

"Can we buy some jerky?" Crystal asked.

"Sure, but don't be late for dinner."

Crystal could see Shawn waiting for her out by Caleb. She hurried out the door grabbing her gray felt cowgirl hat and her ski gloves.

"Hey, city girl, you ready to ride?" Shawn called as she hurried down the steps and past the pines that were scattered in their front lawn.

"Yup," Crystal mimicked.

"Aren't you afraid of Caleb wandering off?" Shawn teased as he looked at the big, gray horse standing by with reins hanging to the ground.

"Are you kidding? He couldn't get along without me." She laughed as she mounted up, "Without me . . . why . . . why . . . he wouldn't have anyone to boss around!"

It was a great day. Fridays were always her favorite, except maybe for some Sundays when God did something special in her life. But this was the kind of day Crystal had a hard time describing to her friends back in southern California.

She and Shawn rode silently down the hill toward the highway and then around toward the state park that adjoined Winchester Lake. The sky was a deep, dark, clear blue that looked as though it could just pull you right off the planet and out into space. The sun, though brilliantly bright, was not in the least warm. The snow from the little storm two days ago had all but melted. Only a thin crust was left in the shady areas among the pines, firs, and tamaracks of the forest.

Crystal's California friends, like Megan and Patty, would think it was freezing. It almost was. But even after only a couple months Crystal had adapted well. Thirty-nine degrees and sunny was considered a good day.

Shawn worked his horse back and forth in an imaginary slalom course. Finally he spoke. "Hey—where are you at? I mean, you look like you're at the National Finals, or something."

"Oh, I guess I was in California." Crystal trotted Caleb up to Shawn.

"Homesick?"

"Oh, no—not at all. But I do miss Megan and Patty. I don't want to be back there. I just wish they could come up here and visit."

"Well, invite them up for Christmas break. Is Patty as cute as Megan?" Shawn teased.

"No way. . . . They are not coming up here." Crystal galloped on up ahead of Shawn. Caleb was feeling good. Crystal could tell that he liked to run in the little crust of snow that dotted the road back to the campgrounds. He held his head high and twisted to see everything in sight.

When they reached the far side of the lake the road ended, and they headed up a little inlet. It was up that very trail that Crystal, Shawn, Betsy Jo, and Brad had found a buried journal that first week of September. But the lake had been drained then. Now water covered the point of their discovery.

When Crystal spoke, she changed the subject. "Shawn, am I too old to learn how to rope?"

"Rope what?" he kidded.

"You know, learn to rope for the team. I feel kind of out of it around Gabrielle and the others. Do you know she is going to enter five events?"

"Maybe six." Shawn added, "If I can't find a guy to rope with me, I'm going to ask Gabrielle. She could be the header and I'll grab the heels."

"What about me?"

"Sure you could learn—but it would take some years before you really get it down. Listen, you're doing great with barrel racing, and learning quickly with pole bending. I think that's enough. But if you want another event, you should try cutting. Caleb's a natural."

"Oh, but I'm just getting used to horses. I don't think I'm ready for trying to understand a steer."

"You don't have to; that horse of yours knows more about steers than you or I ever will. Next week, ask Mr. Duffy if you could learn how to cut. It could be what you're looking for."

They crossed the creek deep in the woods and headed along the far side of it back out to the lake.

"I like the view from back here," Shawn commented as they again reached the lakeshore. "I mean, everything looks so different from this point. The town's so far away you can imagine what it was like at the turn of the century. Just picture a big lumber mill up there on the hill next to the water tower and a long wooden walkway across the road back into town. The Camas Prairie Railroad ran right up to the mill."

"Sounds like you missed out on the good part. Would you have liked to live back then?" Crystal asked.

"Not really," Shawn said thoughtfully. "After all, they had no National High School Rodeo Association and no cute blonde girl from California. Come on, let's race around the lake to the water tower." Shawn hit the flanks of his horse and headed down the trail before Crystal could respond.

Crystal took the challenge and started after him. She didn't expect to catch up, but it was fun just the same. Caleb was fast enough, but the trail was so narrow she didn't want to try to pass. Besides, she had something to think about: *The cute girl from California. So that's what he thinks of me.*

When they rounded the far east end of the lake and started up the embankment, Crystal saw an opportunity to catch Shawn. He was headed down the trail and then up a fairly steep incline She pulled off the trail and pushed Caleb up the hill on an angle and beat Shawn to the top. The race to the water tower was on.

She beat him by a nose. "I won! Not bad for city girl, huh, country boy?" she boasted.

"You took a shortcut!" Shawn protested.

They climbed off their horses and let them wander around in the tall grass and rest. But now the warmth of the horses' breath was making fog in the cold mountain air.

Shawn and Crystal walked around looking at the ruins of what was once a substantial lumber mill. About the only thing left were cement slabs and a few portions of concrete walls.

"What do you know about the mill?" Crystal asked.

15

"You ought to ask my grandad. He knows all about it. All I know is it was still operating in the early '60s. Then some big outfit from down in Boise bought the local owners out. Everyone thought that was great. They figured a big concern like Snake River Lumber Company could keep the mill going—and the jobs for the local people. However, about six months after Snake River bought it, they just up and said they were losing too much money and decided to close it down. I mean, they weren't going to sell it or anything, just close it down and lay everyone off."

"Did they?"

"Yep. Folks around here took it hard. The word was out that Snake River just bought it for a tax loss and planned on closing it from the beginning. 'Course, no one could prove it. Grandad said if they could have proved that's what they did, they would have had to compensate the workers. As it was, not only was eighty percent of the town unemployed, but the value of property fell. You could have bought one of those little mill houses for $300-$500 in the mid-'60s. It really was a shame."

Crystal looked around for enough snow to throw a snowball at Shawn. She scraped up some mushy flakes and continued the conversation. "What happened to all the buildings?"

"Well, the townspeople had just appealed to the government to check out the records of the mill to see if they were entitled to a settlement, when a rare windstorm blew through town and somehow ignited the sawdust pile. Because the mill was already closed down, there was no company fire-fighting equipment around. By the time the Winchester volunteers made it over here, the whole place had burned straight to the ground—office, papers, and all. So that's the end of the matter."

"What did the people do?"

"What could they do but move? Anyway, I'm not sure I got all that right. Ask my grandad, or go look at the old papers in the museum. It's all in there."

One old concrete wall, about ten feet high, leaned out in the air at a forty-five-degree angle. Shawn inched his way to the top and jumped up and down as if it were a teeter-totter, as though he would be able to raise the other end. To his surprise, the top of the wall slowly began to sink, and the bottom end rose out of the mud.

"Crystal! Hey, climb up here. We could lay this wall down," he called.

She climbed up with him and they rocked up and down. They'd just get the big wall to bend over, when its weight would reassert itself and force them back up in the air. They rocked it down once more. Up it shot again. Finally, they rocked and rocked until it stuck on the down-swing. The bottom end of the wall pulled free from the mud that had long encased it and actually was lifted a few feet in the air because of the high center of gravity.

Shawn jumped off the wall. It remained down. "There," he said, "we did our part to help bring down this cement eyesore. Once again the environment has triumphed." He circled around the wall to where the once-buried end now rose out of the mud.

"Crystal!" he shouted.

She turned to look and as she did the wall dislodged from its new home and sank back into the mud. The sudden thrust caused Crystal to catapult off the back side of the wall toward Shawn. He reached up to catch her, and they both tumbled to the ground.

"Shawn Sorensen! Did you do that on purpose?" She stayed for a minute on the ground in his arms where they had fallen.

"Me? Crystal LuAnne Blake! Did *you* do this on purpose?" he laughed.

Crystal stood and brushed herself off. "Well, why did you holler at me?"

"Because under that wall is a safe—one of those big, metal jobbers with the spin dial on the front. It's pushed right down there into the mud. Really!"

"A safe? No kidding, a safe?"

"You got it. Here, come help me push the wall down, and you can see it for yourself."

Shawn and Crystal once again climbed up on the wall and jumped up and down, causing it finally to fall, raising up the downside. This time Shawn stayed on the wall and Crystal hopped off.

"Hurry and look. I don't know how long I can keep this down," Shawn called.

Crystal ran around to the muddy end and peered under the slab. "Hey, there is something under here, and it looks like a safe, all right. Let me crawl under and. . . ."

"No way!" Shawn shouted. "Don't go under there. It's too dangerous. I can't keep this thing up in the air indefinitely. Get that log over there and prop it underneath that end. Maybe we can brace it."

Crystal grabbed the stump and rolled it over to the cement wall. She braced it under the slab. Shawn got off and came around to look.

"This must have been the office," he said. "I guess that wall fell over in the fire and the safe has been pushed down there ever since."

"Let's find out if it's locked," Crystal suggested.

"I don't know; it looks too dangerous under there. That stump might give way."

"Ah, brave country boy—come on, I'll go check it out."

"Crystal, wait!"

But she didn't. On her hands and knees she crawled along the mud under the partially raised end of the wall toward the dial of the old safe.

19

"What am I supposed to do?" she called back.

"Just spin the dial and see if the lever pulls down and the door will open," Shawn guided. "But hurry up and get out of there."

"Hey, the dial spins but the handle won't pull down," Crystal reported. "If we had a crowbar, or something, maybe we could pry it up."

"You aren't prying anything up. . . . Come on." Shawn pulled at her boots.

All her life Crystal had been the hang-back type. Let someone else take the chances. A no-risk life, she called it. But the past few months of life in the mountains had begun to change her. Now when she was just getting to have the freedom that she always wanted, Shawn wouldn't let her have it.

"Come on, mud ball, time to go home," he laughed.

She hadn't thought a lot about what she looked like, but now Crystal looked down at her jeans and jacket to see the smeared mud. She hoped she didn't have any on her face. *Girls look like idiots when they have mud on their faces*, she thought. *Guys look like they have been working hard, but a girl just looks dorky.*

"Do I have any mud on my face?" she asked Shawn as she stood up and tried to rearrange the mess.

"No, not yet, but I can fix that if you want me to." He faked scooping up a handful of mud.

"Shawn Sorensen, you turkey, if you get my

face muddy I'll—I'll—I'll never bake you chocolate chip cookies again!"

"Promise?" he smiled.

They mounted their horses, but Crystal was reluctant to go. "We can't leave that safe. I mean, what if there is something important in there."

"Relax," Shawn replied. "Nothing important could be in there or they would have looked for the safe years ago."

"Can we come back tomorrow and take another look?" she prodded as they headed back out to the highway.

"We've got rodeo team practice in the morning over at Pattersons' arena. Maybe after that. Anyway, it's no big . . . come on, Crystal, not everything in the world is an adventure."

"It sort of is," Crystal thought out loud as they turned west down the road and through some giant ponderosa pines. "What I mean is . . . well, most folks miss the adventures because they either don't look for them, or they fail to recognize what a neat adventure even the little things in life can be. Do you know what I mean?"

"Yeah, a little, but please don't tell anyone. Can you imagine my reputation if the word got out that I actually understood the Lil' Flash?"

"Little Flash?"

"Yeah, it's sort of a joke around school. You and Karla have made a big impact on a high school like Highland. With only 106 students, two, new, suntanned blondes with uptown clothes are bound to get a nickname. Well, someone started calling Karla the California Flash, and so you got stuck being called Little Flash."

They climbed the last hill and headed down the old state highway towards the town's only gas station.

They stopped at the junction. "You want to come over and watch some TV tonight?" Shawn asked.

"Uh . . . well, yeah, maybe later. I'll call you okay?" she stammered.

"Whatever . . . anyway, see you later." He waved and rode off down past Marty's gas station.

She watched for a minute. *I just love it up here. Where else in the world do you say good-bye to a guy and he rides a horse off into the sunset?*

She had been vague about her evening plans because she had a little work to do first. Crystal wasn't about to leave that safe for someone else to discover. She rode up to the back of the house and started rummaging around in her dad's toolshed. She found a small crowbar and a flashlight. Then she rode over to the pasture and dug a rope out of Caleb's tack room.

As she rode by the house, her mom came out to the porch. "Crystal, it's getting too cold. You should come in now. Did you pick up the meat at Norton's?"

"I'm going to get it right now. Be right back," she called.

It was true that she would swing by the store for the meat, but first there was a stop up at the mill site.

When she arrived back at the uplifted wall, it was almost dark. She climbed off Caleb and talked as she worked. She set the flashlight to point in at the safe, then tied one end of the rope to the saddle horn. The other end of the rope she let drag.

"After I see if the crowbar pries it open, I'll wrap that end of the rope around the stump, and we'll pull it out so no one can horn in on our find." Crystal spoke as if she expected Caleb to answer.

He stared at her with his usual, blank, what-in-the-world-is-she-doing-now expression.

Then she crawled once more under the cement slab toward the dimly lit safe. She dragged the little crowbar with her. The space was much tighter than she had imagined. There didn't seem to be any place that she could get a good angle to pry the safe door.

There was a lot less room than before. Then it dawned on her. "The wall is sinking back down!" She jerked around to see the stump slowly sinking into the mud under the force of the wall. Crystal left the crowbar and hurried back out. As she did she could hear the wall shift and come down.

It brushed against her back as she got her head and shoulders out and pulled free to her waist. Then, the weight of the wall pushed her legs right into the mud.

She tried to shove with her arms but she was stuck tight.

Crystal panicked.

2
A CUT ABOVE AVERAGE

"THIS IS NOT HAPPENING TO ME; IT'S REALLY NOT. This is absolutely stupid. I am not stuck in the mud." Crystal muttered and Caleb listened.

Over and over she tired to push her hands into the ground to get some leverage to pull out her legs, but she only succeeded in getting her gloves full of mud.

She noticed the rope that she had dangled around the horn of her saddle. "Maybe. . . ." She developed a plan.

"Caleb—Caleb, old pal. Come here. Come on. Come here!"

The big gray Appy paused to look at her, then calmly munched on some grass. Crystal wanted to scream in frustration. Sometimes she thought he knew exactly what was going on, but he didn't choose to get involved.

"Caleb, you turkey, you get over here right now!" she ordered. "You know I need your help. Don't pretend that you're just some ignorant beast. Now, come here!"

He continued to munch.

Crystal reached back into her jacket and fumbled in the pocket the best she could. "Here, boy

. . . come here. . . . Crystal's got a treat for you."
She pretended to have a bite of carrot or apple.

Now the big gray horse showed some interest.
He sauntered toward Crystal. As he came close,
she lunged for the dropped rope and caught hold
of it with her left hand. She wrapped both of her
muddy gloves around the rope and shot up a
quick prayer. "Lord, this has just got to work,
because if it doesn't I'll have to yell and scream
and somebody will come rescue me and everyone in the whole world will know that I'm a real
klutz. Lord, I'd rather you and me keep that a
secret.

"Giddyup!" she shouted at Caleb.

He didn't move. He bent down to inspect her
gloves instead. He nosed her hands.

"No, no—giddyup! Get! Go on! Go!"

He wasn't in a traveling mood. Caleb lifted his
head and seemed to stare out at the lake. With
her left hand still wrapped around the rope, she
reached out and picked up a twig. She swatted
Caleb's flank.

The big horse bolted back up the hill, and
Crystal felt the rope slip between the fingers of
her muddy glove. She reached over with her
right hand and clung on. Just as she got a good
grip and felt the tension in the rope, Caleb
slowed down. But before he stopped pulling
completely, Crystal managed to get her right leg
free. By placing it against the cement wall, she
pulled her other leg out of the mud.

Her boot was left in the mud, but she quickly retrieved it and put it back on. It was nearly dark now and getting really cold. If it clouded over, it could snow, Crystal thought.

She brushed her hair aside and felt the gritty mud being smeared on her forehead. She coiled up the rope, picked up the flashlight, and thought about the abandoned crowbar under the wall as she climbed up on Caleb.

She rode around the lake and back out on the old highway that led into town, remembering to stop by the market.

She poked her head in the door, not wanting anyone to see how muddy she was. *I hope Travis isn't working in here tonight.* She thought about her classmate whose father owned the meat market. Fortunately for Crystal, Mr. Norton was all alone in the store.

"Er . . . Mr. Norton . . . I need to pick up some meat, and I'm too muddy to come in."

"Crystal! Took a spill, did you?" he replied with a smile.

"Well . . . er, no . . . actually . . . well sort of. And I'd like a package of your home-cured jerky."

Mr. Norton walked over to the door. "Here's the jerky, but your dad was just in to get the meat. He sounded a little worried about you. Man alive, you are about as muddy as anybody I've ever seen. You okay?"

"Thanks. Yeah. It's just—you know, a beauty

treatment. What do you think, is it working?"

"Well, I'd take you around to the side of the shop and hose you off, but you'd freeze," he laughed.

She went back out to climb up on Caleb but before she could he prodded the sack of jerky with his nose.

"Listen, you don't want this. It's jerky. You know, hard and spicy. And besides that, it's expensive."

He continued to shove his nose into her hands until she finally relented. "I love this stuff, so you better eat it all gone," she lectured, sliding a long piece into his mouth. Instantly, Caleb spit out the jerky.

"I knew it! I knew you wouldn't like it. Now you wasted that jerky."

Caleb responded by nosing at the sack once more.

"Oh, no, you don't. No more. Let's get home."

She rode Caleb up the road and watched as the view turned from sunlight to moonlight. Up the road past the gas station, by the church, and then into the pasture. It took her at least fifteen minutes to get Caleb situated for the night. She gave him his dinner and an extra handful of sweet oats. Then she put on his night blanket, wrapped his shins, and left him in the corral.

As Crystal headed toward the back door, she looked up and saw her dad. She didn't wait for him to speak.

"Dad, sorry I'm late. I wanted to go down by the old mill and check out something Shawn and I found this afternoon, but I sort of got stuck in the mud. I guess I blew it, didn't I?"

"Your mother's been pretty worried. You know the rules. We want to know where you're going and when you'll be back. Seems to me you forgot to tell your mother about that."

"You're right. Let me clean up and I'll go talk to Mom."

Dinnertime at the Blake residence that Friday was mainly lecture time. Crystal was the center of concern. She didn't complain, but she didn't have the nerve to tell her parents that she was almost trapped under a wall. The settlement was a strong reinforcement of the rules, and Crystal got to do the evening dishes, which didn't bother her too much. It helped get the mud out from under her fingernails. She did forget to call Shawn until it was almost 10:00. Her mom wouldn't let her call that late, so she spent some time in her room reading.

She tried to figure out what to tell Shawn about the cement wall and safe. If she told him what she did, he'd get mad because he told her it was dangerous. If she didn't, she'd have to explain how a crowbar with her dad's name on it ended up under the wall next to the safe.

She decided just to blurt out the truth. "It's easier," she decided. "Telling lies, or even avoiding the truth, is just too complicated."

Crystal and Gabrielle drove out to Teresa's Saturday morning for team practice. It had been almost two months since Crystal had made the Highland High School rodeo team, and though she wasn't the most experienced, she felt more at ease than at first.

Gabrielle had just gotten her driver's license and drove her dad's pickup while pulling Crystal's horse trailer with both horses inside. Crystal hoped to obtain her license before Christmas. She loved the Idaho law that allowed fourteen-year-olds to drive.

The beautiful blue sky of early morning began to cloud over. Dark gray clouds sailed overhead, only to stack up against the Bitterroot Mountains to the east. Soon the prairie would be covered with them, and they would bring some cold rain, or even snow. The heater in the pickup blasted hot air and the radio crackled and buzzed as it tried to pick up a station from Spokane. Reception up on the four thousand-foot-high Camas Prairie of northern Idaho was not always too clear.

"Gabrielle, would it seem silly if I wanted to learn how to rope?"

"Rope a what?" The dark-skinned girl with the long, jet black braid grinned.

"That's what Shawn said. You know, learn to rope for the team."

"Listen, I think roping is a lot of fun. You

should learn. But it does take a lot of time, and it takes a lot of working with steers and calves if you're going to get rodeo good. You have to sort of know which way they're going before they turn. Anyway, why do you want to learn?"

"Oh, I wanted to go out for another event. Shawn said I should try cutting. What do you think?"

"I think you've got the horse for it. Why not try? Hey, are Karla and Michael getting serious? It seems like they're always together at school."

They pulled into the Patterson ranch and started to unload. "Well, I don't know how serious, but she went out to dinner with his folks last night. At The Ponderosa no less."

"Well, now, that place is classy. I went there once." Gabrielle brushed down her horse and tossed on the saddle blanket. "I ordered this Spanish dinner, and it came out on two huge platters. I mean, I have never eaten so much in my life. How about you and Shawn? Are you guys serious?"

"Well, promise not to tell anyone, but we are going to run off to Winnemucca, Nevada, and get married," Crystal giggled.

"Winnemucca!" Gabrielle mounted her horse. "Have you set the date?" she played along.

"I think in about 10 years," Crystal laughed. "Shawn's a really neat guy, and a great friend and I wish . . . well, let's talk about it sometime." Crystal rode Caleb out into the center of the indoor arena and waved at Dusty Ruthman, another of the girls on the rodeo team.

Crystal liked being on the rodeo team. It was hard for her to explain to her folks. It was next to impossible to explain to her southern California friends. The nearest thing she could say was that it all made her feel so at home. She felt relaxed and comfortable up on Caleb. She felt at peace with herself and everyone when they put in their paces and rounded the barrels. *It's just who I am*, she thought.

The Pattersons' arena was great for practice, but Crystal liked being outside better. Outside, the dust didn't hang in the air quite as long, and the voices didn't bounce back at her. And she loved the nice breeze in the late summertime. It didn't seem quite right to ride a horse indoors. It felt like riding in a box.

At one end of the arena, the boys in the riding events warmed up on a black bucking machine. Mrs. Patterson led in some goats for the girls to practice tying.

"Maybe I should learn to throw a goat and tie it," Crystal said to herself as she rode Caleb around the three-barrel cloverleaf pattern another time.

Although the official rodeo team competition didn't begin until spring, the Highland High team participated in some practice rodeos. Next week they'd go to Pendleton, Oregon, for competition with the legendary Pendleton High School team. Then they had a rodeo in Spokane with six different teams competing. And right before Christmas they traveled up to Kalispell, Montana, for a rodeo in the big Bitterroot Valley Arena.

Crystal really wanted to be able to enter three events. She knew there were eleven events in high school rodeos (not counting the queen contest). In order to be five deep in every event, it required most everyone to enter three events. For some, like Gabrielle or Shawn, that posed no problem. But for Crystal . . .

She rode over to the north side of the arena and watched the girls tie the goats. It didn't look too hard. "All you've got to do is ride hard about fifteen yards," Crystal mused, "fly off your horse, catch and throw the goat, tie three legs with a 'piggin' string', and stand clear." Crystal liked it all but the throwing and tying part.

Shawn had been doing some roping, but now rode up to visit with Crystal. "Hey, cowgirl, hope you didn't get worried last night when I wasn't home. My folks wanted us all to go down to Riggins, so I wasn't there when you called," he explained.

"Oh, well . . . actually . . . I . . . I did something really dumb and I got muddy and sort of in trouble. . . ."

"You didn't go back over to the lake and try to dig out that safe, did you." he accused.

33

"Well, sort of. . . . I mean, you'll find out anyway. I went back with a crowbar and climbed under to force open the safe. But then a stump started giving way in the mud, and I tried to climb out. But the wall slid down and pinned my legs and Caleb had to pull me out and I was a muddy mess . . . and kind of cold, and a little scared, and late for dinner. And if you say one word about I-told-you-so, Shawn Sorensen, I'll hit you with my whip!"

"You really know how to sweet-talk a guy." Shawn cowered. "Does this mean our safe-digging expedition is off?"

"Frankly, I'm not very interested today," Crystal sighed. "Maybe we should wait for spring."

"I am kind of busy today," Shawn added. "Teresa asked me if I would help her practice."

"Practice what?" The idea of Shawn and Teresa together froze Crystal to attention.

"Well, Teresa's going to sing next Friday in the school assembly, and she asked me to play the guitar."

"She asked you? And you said yes?"

"Hey, why not? With you and her being such good friends I figured it was like doing you a favor."

"Good friendships can end quickly, cowboy. Remember that," Crystal tried to say lightheartedly.

"I knew you wouldn't mind." Shawn was

watching as the goats were herded out of the arena. "They're bringing in the steers for the cutting practice. Come on, let's help."

Crystal followed Shawn and some others as they brought in the small cows. She really liked horses, but reserved her opinion about cows. She absolutely knew she did not like bulls. Calves were all right, as long as she didn't have to flip one over and tie its legs. And steers—well, they didn't seem all that interesting or bright.

"You've got to try cutting today," Shawn called out.

"Maybe so. Wouldn't be the first time I tried something I know nothing about." She rode over with Shawn and the others who waited in line. "Go over the rules with me again."

"Well, you just walk Caleb into the herd slowly and select the animal, then cut it out of the herd as smooth as possible and drive it to the middle of the arena. You try to keep it from rejoining the others. Actually, Caleb will do all the work. They judge you from sixty to eighty. If you've got the horse, it's a great event. You give him the lead, and you get all the glory."

"I don't know. What if I fall off and get trampled by the cows?"

"It will definitely mess up your hair," Shawn laughed. "Listen, no one gets hurt cutting. Maybe Caleb's not too good at it, but you won't get hurt."

"Caleb not good? Hey, remember him herding

that guy down in the Salmon River? Mr. Kirkland said he's a cutting horse. I'm just not sure I'm a cutting girl."

"Are you going to try or not?"

"Yeah, well, I guess."

"All right! Hey, Dusty, wait up. Crystal's going to give it a try."

Suddenly, Crystal had that sinking feeling again. It used to be a common occurrence. B.I., that was. Before Idaho. But then she and Megan raced the stagecoach, and she and Caleb captured the con man down on the Salmon, and her first rodeo. . . . There were days when she completely forgot how worry about failure used to dominate her life.

This was not one of those days. While she rode out to the center of the arena she thought, *I'm just a California girl who should be back home watching MTV or going to the beach or something. I really don't know anything about this.*

Then she remembered what Grandpa Northstar told her and Gabrielle once. "Talk to your horse. Let him know what is expected."

"Well, Caleb. You see, this is your event. I mean, they don't judge me too much, but they judge you. Now, I can't tell you what to do, but let's get one of those steers out here and keep it in the center. Show them what a real cow pony is like." She leaned over and rubbed his neck.

Crystal dug her boot heels into Caleb's sides, and they galloped toward the herd kept in place

36

by several riders. Crystal remembered that Shawn emphasized the importance of style and performance. Her eye was immediately drawn to a black-and-white steer, since most of the herd were white-faced red Herefords. Caleb didn't hesitate to plunge in, and once he was sure which one Crystal aimed for, he took charge.

Only once before had Crystal sensed how excited Caleb could be. His body quivered, his eyes flashed, and he snorted and pranced as he pushed the black-and-white out of the herd. The steer twisted to the right, then to the left, trying to circle the horse and rejoin the others. Caleb anticipated each move. He turned one step ahead of the steer each time.

With great ease and efficiency he pushed the black-and-white to the middle of the arena. Several times it tried to break around Caleb on a dead run. Each time he was there to stop the retreat.

Finally, the steer in utter frustration stood perfectly still in the center of the arena, resigned to being singled out, and just bawled for help.

Only then did Crystal hear the cheers from her teammates.

"All right, Lil' Flash!" someone called. It sounded like Teresa Patterson.

The team coach, Mr. Duffy, called her over to the rail. Caleb didn't want to leave the steer, but finally Crystal kicked him hard enough and reined him over. The black-and-white cantered happily back to the others.

"Crystal. That was an excellent performance for the first time out; Caleb's quite a horse," Mr. Duffy complimented.

"Yeah, well, I had forgotten, but Mr. Kirkland said he was a good cutting horse."

"Kirkland's been noted for understatements. Listen, Crystal, I want you to turn around and do that one more time. This time I want you to bring out that white-faced yearling that's hanging around its momma. See it over by the fence?" Mr. Duffy pointed toward the back of the arena.

"What do you think, Caleb? You ready for another go-round?" It was a superfluous question and Crystal knew it. She had a feeling that Caleb would be out there cutting cattle until he dropped, if anyone would let him.

They reentered the herd with ease. Caleb was definitely not spooked by milling cattle. When she got him to the yearling, Caleb sensed the problem even better than she did. The calf determined not to get so much as an inch away from his mother, and his mother seconded the motion. She got indignant about this intrusion on family life. The commotion caught Crystal by surprise, but it didn't phase Caleb. He cut out the calf, leaving the complaining mother behind in a matter of seconds.

The hysterical calf bawled and turned and

bolted and dodged and refused to be predictable. But nothing fazed Caleb. He acted like a horse that had been through it all before.

Once, on television, Crystal watched a program all about sheep dogs and what great herders they are. She never imagined that she'd been riding a big gray horse that seemed to be a natural of the same order.

Caleb kept it up until Mr. Duffy shouted out, "Come on, let the little fella go. He's about to have a heart attack."

Crystal rode over to the rail, and Mr. Duffy called the whole team together.

"Now, we've got the rodeo down at Pendleton coming up. I don't want you spreading yourself too thin, so I'm going to limit most of you to your three top events. The next week I want you to concentrate on just those events. You all know that there isn't much chance of us upsetting Pendleton, but some of you ought to bring home some prizes. Just like other years, I'm appointing some captains in different events. Now, don't take it too personal, but I'll need someone to help see that the contestants are organized and ready to go.

"Here's how it lines up: Travis takes the saddle bronc riders; Bill Emmert, the bull riders; Leon, the bareback riders. Now, I don't usually double up, but you fellas know we got ourselves one super roper here, so Shawn is going to captain both the team roping and calf roping. Tony will take the steer wrestlers. I'm putting Staci on goat tying, Dusty on breakaway roping. Teresa will head up the pole benders, and Gabrielle gets the honors for barrel racing. Coming into today I was still a little worried about that cutting slot. Not many of you spend much time herding cattle, and we've been a bit weak.

"Most of you haven't been around long enough to really appreciate what just happened out there in the arena. I've been in rodeo since I was six years old. I've been coaching and judging high school rodeo since it came to Idaho in 1959. What you just saw out there was the closest to an eighty that you'll ever see. There's not a rodeo in the country that wouldn't have been first place. We've got some team points sewed up right there. This year's cutting captain is going to be . . ."

"Lil' Flash!" Gabrielle shouted.

Mr. Duffy smiled. "Yep. You're the one, Crystal. Now, keep that horse of yours healthy, you hear?"

3

THE RETURN OF THE MUD MONSTERS

NOT ONCE IN HER LIFE HAD CRYSTAL LuANNE Blake been a leader at anything. In the shadow of a very proficient sister, she'd been happy to tag along, with Karla in charge. All through school she enjoyed being around others who were decisive and forceful leaders. Her role always seemed to be someone's first assistant. In junior high she'd served as vice-president or secretary of about every organization she joined. But never president, chairperson, captain, or queen.

To most fourteen-year-old girls in the country being the cutting captain of the Highland High School rodeo team wouldn't be much. Maybe the school just had a little over 100 students. Maybe there were only a couple dozen kids on the team. Maybe it was the weakest event on the team. That wasn't important.

Crystal thought that she was going to cry when she realized that she would be one of the team captains. It meant she was somebody on her own. It had nothing to do with her dad being an author, nothing to do with a big sister, nothing to do with her trying to pretend to be something she wasn't.

But, it did have a lot to do with her horse.

When practice was over she rode out to the trailers with Shawn and Gabrielle. "Maybe they should have made Caleb captain," she mentioned as they unsaddled the horses.

Shawn put his arm around her shoulder. "Listen, Crys, you've got to have a rider that can bring out the best in a cutting horse. You're that rider. You and Caleb. From the time you got on him back in August at Kamiah you two have hit it off."

"He's right," Gabrielle continued. "You're the one he wants to impress. Don't let Caleb's indifferent look fool you. He's just like a big puppy trying to please. Some people I know have been looking their whole life for just the right horse. And you got yours right off. How's that for luck?"

"Hey, well, thanks, you guys. Anyway, congratulations. A double captain, that's neat, Shawn." Crystal finished putting the big gray into the trailer.

"I think Mr. Duffy wanted to make Shawn captain of about six events, but I guess that was out. Anyway, I thought Teresa would be in the barrels, after all I'm . . ." Gabrielle didn't complete the sentence.

"You're a national finals quality barrel racer," Shawn added.

"Thanks . . . you guys are really neat friends. I'm so glad you both moved up to Winchester this year." Gabrielle smiled.

"Hey," Crystal interrupted. "You guys want to come over tonight for popcorn and a movie? Dad's rented one for the VCR."

"As long as it's not a western," Gabrielle winced.

Crystal looked surprised. "You don't like westerns?"

"Nah, my side always loses." Gabrielle laughed.

Crystal sensed the laugh had a hollow sound to it, not like the Gabrielle she knew. "No western. It's that old Humphrey Bogart flick, *Casablanca*. What about it?"

"I'll be there," Gabrielle said.

"Yeah, me, too," Shawn agreed, "as long as I can get through playing the guitar for Teresa in time."

Gabrielle and Crystal rode back to Winchester in silence most of the way. "What's this about playing the guitar for Teresa?" Gabrielle finally said.

"Oh," Crystal explained, "she asked Shawn to accompany her for the assembly on Friday. It's no big."

"She asked him?"

"Yeah, so what?"

"Nothing. I guess. But as long as I've known Teresa she's always had Paul Judd play for her. Paul lives in that green house right down from Teresa's. You know the one with the giant satellite dish? I wonder what's wrong with Paul?"

"Well, I'm not going to let you make me jealous. I refuse to be jealous. Shawn and I are very good friends, that's all. And he can certainly accompany anyone he chooses. Did I ever tell you about the time he sang a song to me at the . . .?"

"Do you believe all that garbage that just came out of your mouth?" Gabrielle interrupted. "You, who a mere ten minutes ago had Shawn's arm around your shoulder and you blushing like a redskin, now try telling me that you are just 'good friends'?"

"Ah, well, it does sound a little phony, I guess," Crystal admitted.

"Phony? Phony! It's a crock of buffalo chips," Gabrielle howled.

"Yeah, you're right. If Teresa makes one move for Shawn, I'll . . ."

"Yeah, you told me before."

Gabrielle helped Crystal unload Caleb. "I'll keep the trailer at my place until tonight," she called to Crystal as she jumped back into the truck and headed home.

Saturday afternoon Crystal cleaned her room and pored over her never-ending Spanish homework. Karla bounded downstairs and into Crystal's room with a backwards dive on her bed.

"Hey, don't mess it up. I haven't passed final inspection yet," Crystal complained.

Karla ignored the protest. "Well," she said, "I

just had a two-hour phone conversation with Michael."

"And?"

"I broke up with him."

"You what?" Crystal put down the Spanish book and came over to the bed.

"Yeah. I broke up with him. Really," Karla sighed.

"Wow. What happened? Did he, ah . . . I mean . . . wow . . . how . . . come?" Crystal stammered.

"I really feel crummy about it—it's my fault, you know." Karla stared at the ceiling, then closed her eyes.

"Your fault? Did you . . . well . . . well, I mean . . ."

Karla continued to talk as if Crystal had not spoken at all. "You see, Michael is a neat guy. And wow, is he cute! But I went out with him because all the girls at school wanted to go out with him, and when he asked me that first week of school I sort of, you know, wanted to show off. Well, last night I finally realized a couple things when I was with his folks."

Crystal laid back on the bed with her sister and listened as Karla continued. "I've always made it a rule, just like Mom and Dad tell us, not to go out with someone you wouldn't want to marry."

"You wouldn't want to marry Michael?"

"He's a great guy, except for one area. He's a spiritual flake. I mean, he claims he's a Christian, but he just doesn't know what that means. Last night I realized that neither he nor his parents really know the Lord. That's just one standard I'm not going to compromise on. Marriage is tough enough when you have everything going for you, but I'm not about to start out in the hole. I've just been letting my pride push me on. So, I broke up."

"You told him all that?"

"Not exactly. How do you tell a guy like Michael Flannery he's a spiritual flake and you've just been leading him on? I don't know, Crys—that's why it took me two hours. I guess I just beat around the bush a lot. Anyway, I know I did the right thing, and I think I'm going to cry."

She got up to get a tissue. Crystal also got up and hugged her sister. "You're a great sister, Karla."

"What's that for?"

"Because you keep reminding me what's important. Sometimes I forget."

Karla started up the stairs to the living room. "Well, at least some of the seniors will be happy not to have the California Flash to deal with," Crystal called.

"California Flash, huh? Is that what I'm called?" Karla turned on the stairway.

"Yeah, well, it beats being known as Lil' Flash," Crystal laughed.

Crystal liked *Casablanca*, but halfway into it

46

the VCR broke down. So Crystal, Shawn, and Gabrielle ended up talking their way through three batches of popcorn.

She and Shawn told Gabrielle all about the safe that was under the wall at the old mill.

"Well, I think we ought to go dig it up," Gabrielle encouraged. "Maybe it's antique and worth something."

"I don't know." Crystal added, "Shawn, Betsy Jo, Brad, and I dug around out in the slime one time and didn't end up with anything more than being late to Gretchen's wedding. To tell you the truth, I'm still trying to wash the mud off from yesterday. I'd really like to find out about that safe, but I don't want to do the digging."

"Okay. Let's take one more look at it tomorrow afternoon. Why don't I call Brad and Betsy Jo, and we can reinstate the Lapwai Meadow Exploratory Committee?" Shawn suggested.

"All right, but I'm not getting muddy!" Crystal insisted.

By the time Crystal got out of the house the next day after church and Sunday dinner, it was after two. The others had already arrived and had once again raised the big wall. This time they propped four logs under it, exposing the top of the safe and the Blake family crowbar.

"Hi, Betsy Jo, where's Brad?" Crystal greeted.

"He couldn't come up today, but he demanded one-quarter of all the money we find," Betsy Jo laughed.

"One-quarter? Now it's only one-fifth. Only it's no show, no share," Crystal kidded as she got off Caleb and inspected their work. "Gabrielle is a new team member," she announced.

"Great! I was afraid that you and I would have to do all the digging again!"

"Again!" Shawn crawled out from under the wall where he had unsuccessfully been trying his hand at safe opening.

"Well, I told Shawn I'm not getting back under there in the mud. I almost got stuck but good Friday afternoon. Hey, listen up, I've got some important news."

"Like why you were late getting out here?" Shawn chided.

"Sort of. We had company for lunch after church, so I couldn't leave right away, at least not until after the blueberry cheesecake."

"Yeah, well," Betsy Jo laughed, "it's mean, dirty, rotten work, but someone has to eat the cheesecake."

"All right, you guys, this is really big news! You see, Mrs. Milton, the head of the history department at Lewis-Clark College, came over to the house."

"Hey, hey! Wowie zowie! That is big news," Gabrielle kidded. The others joined in the laughter. "Who's Mrs. Milton?"

"Okay, turkeys, I shouldn't even tell you. But Mrs. Milton is the one who wrote about the history of Lewis County. She had a section in her book about the Snake River Lumber Company closing down the Winchester Mill. I asked her about it, and she said that while the mill was obviously slowing down, most folks thought it should have lasted another ten to twenty years. That's why they got mad thinking that Snake River bought it knowing all along they would shut it down and write it off. Lots of folks lost their jobs, and some even their homes and property.

"She said that they banded together and were going to go to court about the shutdown, but that all the papers that could have substantiated their position were in the company safe that burned up in the fire. Did you get that? This might be *the safe*."

"No foolin'?" Shawn looked surprised.

"I told you I had some news."

"Well," he continued, "I have some news, too. There's no way I can get that safe door open down there. I think we need to dig out the whole safe."

"I'm not digging," Crystal insisted.

"Well, I guess it won't hurt me." Gabrielle grabbed up a shovel and crawled underneath. "I've got to take a bath tonight anyway."

"I hope it's not as bad as it looks." Shawn grabbed the heavy maddox that he had brought and joined Gabrielle. From underneath the raised end of the wall he instructed the others. "Crys, you ride Caleb right up on that end of the wall and just stand him there. With the extra weight, there's no way these logs will sink into the mud and let the wall down on us.

"Betsy Jo, ride out towards the forest and get a couple of fifteen-foot, four-inch-around black pine poles. If we get this out, we will have to travois it up to town."

Crystal regretted she'd made the big deal about not shoveling. While she sat on Caleb and stared out at the lake, Gabrielle and Shawn dug, visited, and laughed under the other end of the wall.

Betsy Jo returned before long, dragging a couple long poles which she had lashed to either side of her saddle.

"Betsy Jo, would you believe that I'm one of the rodeo team captains?" Crystal blurted out.

"Of the nondigging event," Shawn called out from below.

Crystal couldn't see the whole project, but she could tell they were digging a ramp of some kind.

Finally Shawn, Gabrielle, and Betsy Jo emerged from under the wall. "You know, in the summertime, the dirt under that wall would have been too dry and hard to dig," Shawn reminded them. "Now, time for a little team ropin', Gabrielle. Let's see if we can slide the safe up. Betsy Jo, knock those logs out as soon as the safe gets to the edge. They'll be in the way. Crys, you keep the wall up until we get it out."

50

Both Shawn's and Gabrielle's horses were used to keeping a rope taut. As they encouraged the horses, Crystal could tell the safe was starting to slide.

"Come on—giddyup—come on," Gabrielle coaxed with new vigor.

Betsy Jo knocked out one of the blocks to let the safe slide by. Crystal dismounted Caleb and witnessed the top of the safe come into view. Betsy Jo shoved another brace aside.

All at once the safe popped free, and the two remaining braces started to falter. With the rumble of the cement wall beneath his feet, Caleb climbed off the far end, leaving Crystal alone. She cheered the recovery of the safe.

Then, the props collapsed at the low end of the wall, and it teetered back down on the now-empty hole. The end Crystal stood on shot up in the air. She was propelled off and landed face-down in a pile of mud that had been dug out from around the safe.

"I knew it! I just knew something like this would happen! Why me?" In her best theatrical voice she wailed up at the sky, "Why me, Lord? Why does mud hate me?"

But even a muddy face couldn't dampen Crystal's spirits. They had recovered the safe.

"Well, open it up." Betsy Jo directed her words toward Shawn.

"Open it? If I could have opened it, we wouldn't have needed to pull it out of there. Set those travois poles down. Let's get that two-ton monster lashed to them Indian style. The travois was always the Indian mode of moving camp, right, Gabrielle?" Shawn prompted.

"Don't ask me; we always use a pickup," she informed him.

Shawn and Gabrielle, being the ropers in the crowd, laid their ropes on the ground and pushed the safe over on its side on top of the ropes. Then they tied the ropes to the two poles with crisscrosses and well-placed knots.

"Now," Shawn commanded, "when we hoist the poles down there at the long end, we'll raise this thing off the ground. Then we can tie each of these poles to a saddle and we'll drag that dude up the hill and over to Crystal's house. It's the closest."

Caleb and Spade, Shawn's horse, were selected to do the pulling. The ropes stretched and the poles sagged when they lifted the safe in place, but it did swing off the ground. Very slowly they rounded the lake and aimed for Crystal's.

Crystal looked around at the others as they made a turn up Camas Drive. "You know what? This is weird. Look at us, four kids riding horses and dragging a big black safe. And nobody even notices. It just fits Winchester, Idaho. You try this in southern California, you'd be arrested and thrown into jail within minutes. I love Idaho!"

"Yeah, well, it's funny," Shawn said. "I love it,

too, and I've never ever been to California."

Camas Drive in Winchester, Idaho, was like all the other residential streets—a gravel, narrow roadway. The bounce of the log poles over the rocks began to shake the safe loose from the ropes, and one of the poles cracked. So, by the time they finally made it to the Blake home, they were dragging the safe on the gravel.

They hauled it over to the grass at the edge of Crystal's front yard and pulled the ropes loose. Try as they might, they could not get any type of pry bar caught in the door in order to force it open. Gabrielle, Crystal, Betsy Jo, and Shawn all tried their hand at spinning the combination dial, but to no avail.

"On television, they always shoot the lock and it pops right open," Betsy Jo suggested, half serious.

"I can go get my dad's gun," Gabrielle offered.

"Isn't that a little radical?" Crystal didn't know if they really meant it or not.

Shawn sat down on the raised deck sidewalk and scratched his head. "I know, let me go get a sledgehammer and a chisel. Maybe we can bust the lock clear off. With all the rust on the outside, you'd think it would be pretty easy.

The chisel rang out with every smash. Its sound echoed through the treetops. But the hammer merely bounced off the chisel, and by the sixth whack, the chisel handle broke.

"Crystal," Shawn said as he stood up to stare

at the broken chisel, "did you say there was a book written about the mill?"

"I think it's about all of Winchester, not just the mill. But I know it had a section about the mill, too. Why?"

"Well," Shawn spoke softly and slowly. "Maybe the safe's combination is in the book."

Betsy Jo countered, "Hey, they don't put safe combinations in books."

"Not on purpose," Shawn continued, "but I saw this television show the other day, and some rich lady made her safe combination be the same as her Beverly Hills address. Maybe we could discover some clue like that."

"That sounds like a tedious long shot," Betsy Jo added. "There's got to be something quicker."

"I say shoot it and get it out of its misery," Gabrielle countered.

"Is that safe?" Crystal didn't think she was going to like anything with guns in it.

"This is safe, paleface," Gabrielle joked, pointing to the big, black metal box. She climbed up on her horse and hollered back at them as she rode off. "I'll be right back with the ammunition."

Upon Gabrielle's return they planned the strategy. One of them would pull the trigger while the others hid behind distant trees. The girls all volunteered to hide behind the trees.

Shawn, with gun in hand, stared at the safe. He called out to the girls, "This always looks easy on television. Now watch out for a ricocheting bullet." He stepped to one side, revaluated where to shoot the safe's combination lock, and then he held the gun with both hands, pointed it toward the safe, and said, "Let's hope this does something."

A loud explosion trumpeted through the treetops. Shawn checked the lock and shrugged his shoulders at the girls. Suddenly Karla raced out the front door shouting, "Do you guys have any idea what you just did?"

4
CAN ANYONE UNDERSTAND BOYS?

KNEW IT! I KNEW IT WASN'T SAFE! KARLA, WHAT happened?" Crystal shouted.

"Look!" Karla pointed to the top of the Blake home, and the quartet stared up at an inverted, swinging television aerial. "You almost shot our antenna off!"

"Ur . . . well, Gabrielle, so much for shoot-'em-ups," Shawn stammered. "Here, you'd better take this back to your house."

"It ruined the TV reception, huh?" Betsy Jo nodded at Karla.

"Worse. It made channel 13 come in from Spokane clear as a bell. Allyson is in heaven and I'll never get to watch anything else."

"Channel 13? The all-cartoon channel? It's always been too fuzzy to watch," Crystal commented.

"Well, it's not now. Hey, you'd better get that thing off the lawn before Mom and Dad come home. They went to Lewiston to a meeting and will be back any minute." Karla returned to the house.

"Off the lawn?" Betsy Jo looked around, "We can't even budge it, so let's try to figure out some sane way of getting it open."

"I think best with french fries and a milk shake," Shawn added. "Let's put up the horses and meet down at the Inn."

By the time Betsy Jo and Crystal joined them, Shawn and Gabrielle were already seated at a booth by the front window.

"Don't they make a wonderful couple?" Betsy Jo teased.

"Watch it, Sorensen," Crystal mumbled under her breath. "One more comment like that and I'll write you out of my will."

"Hey, Crystal, sit down, we already ordered for you," Garielle laughed. "The special of the day: liver and onions."

"Yeah," Shawn added, "it's a milk shake."

"Say, you guys, Karla had an idea about opening the safe. Why don't we call a locksmith? You know, one of those guys you call to come fix the locks on your house."

"Who has locks on their doors?" Betsy Jo replied.

"I suppose we could," Shawn pondered. "But it might cost a bundle to get someone to drive up here from Lewiston. Anyway, I think we ought to handle it ourselves."

"Well, I hope you've got an idea for getting that thing off my front yard. It looks tacky," Crystal complained.

"Tacky. Why I thought it was in style. Maybe you could make a planter out of it," Betsy Jo suggested with a touch of sarcasm.

"I wonder if you can check out a book on how to, you know, open a safe," Crystal proposed.

"Sure," Gabrielle added, *Bankrobbing Made Easy.*"

"Or, *Elementary Cat Burglary Tools*," Shawn laughed.

"Well, it wouldn't hurt to check," Crystal huffed, tired of the humor. "What time do we practice tomorrow?"

"Four to six, just like last week." Gabrielle played with some french fries as she talked.

"Well, I am going to the library tomorrow before practice. Surely they will have something to help us open a safe." Crystal spoke with finality.

"Speaking of library, I've got homework." Gabrielle popped up out of the booth. "I better get going. . . . See you guys tomorrow."

Shawn stretched, then announced, "I've got to get to the grocery store before it closes. We'll figure something out tomorrow."

Betsy Jo and Crystal sat alone at the booth. Only a couple men sat drinking coffee and visiting at the long counter.

"Betsy Jo . . . I wondered," Crystal hesitated. "I mean, do you know a lot about boys?"

"Hah! Know about boys? Me, know about boys? Do fish swim? Do birds fly? Do dogs bark? Let me tell you something, I know about boys." Betsy Jo put on her best pose.

58

"Good," Crystal laughed, "tell me everything you know."

"How much time do you have?" Betsy Jo giggled.

"How much time do you need?" Crystal brushed back her blonde hair and peered over her milk-shake glass.

"Oh, about five minutes." Betsy Jo laughed, "You ask *me* about boys? I mean, you're the kid that grew up in southern California. You're the one who came to town with the super tan and the flashing smile. You're supposed to tell me about boys. All I know is that there are some tall ones and some short ones. There are some plain ones and some great-looking ones. There are some smart ones and some not-so-smart ones. There are some strong ones and some weak ones. And if you find one that is tall, great looking, smart, and strong, you'd better grab that dude before the homecoming queen nabs him."

"That's it?" Crystal smiled.

"What else did you want to know?"

"Well, I wondered how serious does a sophomore boy want to get with a freshman girl? I mean, you know, Shawn and me?"

"I guess that depends on the guy. But I know Shawn really likes you."

"Oh, yeah, how do you know that?"

" 'Cause you are the only girl he's ever spent more than ten minutes with in his whole life. Believe me, I'm his cousin," Betsy Jo counseled.

"Does he ever talk about me?"

"Hey, I live in Nezperce, remember?" Betsy Jo shrugged. "So I don't see him very much. But a couple weeks ago we were over here visiting Grandpa, and someone teased Shawn about his new blonde girl friend."

"What did he say?"

"Nothing."

"Nothing?"

"Yeah, but that was quite a bit for him. Normally he'd spend twenty minutes denying that he had a girl friend. This time he just said nothing, sort of silent agreement—I think." Betsy Jo continued, "What's troubling you, anyway?"

"Well, I really like Shawn, and we've gotten to be really good friends. And that's great. I mean, I don't think I'm ready for anything more than that. But someday when I'm older, like Karla, I'd like to get more serious with him, but in the meantime I don't want him going out with other girls. See, I want us to . . ."

"Hey, I understand. You sort of want to own him and save him all for yourself." Betsy Jo wasn't laughing anymore.

"Dumb, huh?"

"Uh . . . well . . . not dumb, but sort of impossible. I mean I don't think you can be that possessive in a nonserious relationship."

"Yeah, that's what I was afraid you would say."

"Well, at least you have something to think

about. Man, things at Nezperce are dead as nails. I haven't seen Brad in three weeks, either. Riggins is just too far away. You know what I heard? I heard Terri Biggers is chasing Brad. Since there's no Shawn to chase, she just moves in on Brad," Betsy Jo pouted.

"Listen, I've got to go, too. Let me know when you figure out how to open the safe, and I'll come back over. Remember, one-fourth of all the loot inside is mine."

Suddenly Crystal sat all alone. It felt strange. For the first time in weeks she was by herself. Everyday had been one hectic event after another. It felt nice to sit for a minute alone, and then walk up the road to her house.

As she passed by the church, she remembered her struggle to understand her feelings about Shawn. "Lord," she whispered, "help me not to worry so much about my relationship with Shawn."

That night Crystal dreamed about teaching little children how to ride and take care of horses. She enjoyed the dream.

Monday was cold and cloudy, but it didn't snow. Crystal was grateful for that. She loved the snow, but knew it caused problems for many driving to and from school. *God should allow it only to snow at night when we are all in bed*, she thought. *Or at least only on weekends or holidays when people can stay at home.*

61

She had Karla let her off at the library after school. Crystal pushed open the heavy, wooden door and loosened her wool scarf. "Mrs. Nelson, where are the 'How to' books?" she asked.

"Well, what we have will be over on the east wall, toward the corner. What do you want, how to remove a safe from your yard?"

"You heard about the safe we found?"

"Oh, yes, everyone in town knows about it. We're all curious about what's inside."

Crystal perked up, "Yeah, me, too! I was wondering if there was a book about how locks and safes are made. You know, so we could figure out how to open it."

Mrs. Nelson picked up a computer printout and studied through the green sheets. "Of course we don't have anything like that here, but I can get it if they have anything in Lewiston. Here's one called *Basic Locksmithing*. Does that sound close?"

"Sure! I mean it might help. How soon can you get it?" Crystal checked her watch and thought about the chores she needed to do before rodeo team practice.

"If they have it in the library, I could have it by Friday."

"Great! Could you order it for me?"

"Sure, and here's a book I think you might enjoy reading: *The Economic Decline of Northern Idaho: 1950-1975*.

"What do I want with that?" Crystal asked.

"Chapter 11 is titled 'Whatever Happened to Winchester Milling Company?' It tells about the shutdown, the fire, and the legal hassles. You know, it might be some of the story is still in the safe."

"Hey, that's exactly what Mrs. Milton said!" Crystal remembered the conversation with the history teacher.

"Well, read it for yourself." Mrs. Nelson handed Crystal the heavy, paperback brown book.

Crystal read through the chapter quickly as she hurried home and did her chores with Caleb. She barely had finished when Gabrielle pulled up, ready to go to practice.

It was starting to snow a little by the time they arrived at the Pattersons' indoor arena. It seemed to Crystal like a nice day to sit by the fireplace and look out.

"Anyway," Crystal picked up the conversation that she had begun on the way over, "this guy Gerhard, who wrote the book, said that Snake River Lumber had made such a profit in selling lumber to tract home builders in California they needed to have a loss in order to save on taxes. He claims by buying the Winchester Mill for 1.2 million and folding it up, they saved over six million in taxes."

"That's weird." Gabrielle mounted up. "They throw away a million in order to make five. Anyway, it was their money. They could do whatever they wanted to, right.

"Sort of." Crystal climbed up on Caleb and rode with Gabrielle. "But this guy who wrote the book says there's a 1908 Idaho law that says if a mill or a mine closes down while it is profitable to continue, the workers deserve fair compensation for relocation and retraining. I guess mills used to open and close so often it played confusion on the economy of this area.

"Anyway, here's the point. Just like Mrs. Milton said the other day. The mysterious fire at the mill destroyed all the papers proving whether the mill was still a going venture. Snake River Lumber said that all the papers were in the company safe, which was lost somewhere in the fire or the cleanup operations that followed."

"But that was twenty-five years ago. Does the law still apply after all those years?" Gabrielle asked.

"This guy wrote the book in 1977, and said it was still valid then. I don't know about now," Crystal said.

"We've just got to get that thing open," Gabrielle concluded.

"And we've got to get ready for the big test at Pendleton High." Crystal broke away from Gabrielle and ran Caleb through the barrel-racing course.

Of the three events that Crystal practiced, barrel racing was still her favorite. From the first day down on the river at Gretchen's ranch, she had loved the feel of a great big, powerful, muscular horse under her pushing through a course at top speed and flying across the finish line.

Pole bending interested girls like Teresa, Crystal figured, because it looked more graceful. *And you get to be out in front of the crowd for a longer period of time—at least four or five seconds more, anyway.*

Pole bending reminded Crystal of ice skating. There was the sprint to the far end of the arena, a slalom around six brightly painted poles, then back around the poles once more and race home.

She enjoyed the cutting horse competition, mainly because it was a time to show off Caleb, and it looked like it might be something she could win.

But nothing could compare to the teamwork feeling of barrel racing. The pattern, the turns, the bursts of speed—even the dust that hung in the air of the indoor arena—it all added to the fun. That afternoon Crystal knew two things. As long as Caleb was healthy she had a good chance of winning some silver in cutting, but she would never really feel complete until she won in barrel racing.

"Lil' Flash!"

She turned to see Teresa Patterson riding up. "Crystal, can you go into Lewiston on Friday afternoon? We need to pick up some team shirts, and Mr. Duffy said it was up to us captains. If we could find something new before the Pendleton Rodeo, it would be sharp."

"Sure, I guess Friday is all right," Crystal agreed.

"And thanks for letting me borrow Shawn to accompany me on my song. Boy, have you heard him sing? I mean he's really . . . really . . . well, you know." Teresa winked.

Crystal stopped smiling.

Teresa rode off to visit with Dusty, and Crystal spurred Caleb back around the barrels. "Wink at me?" she fumed to herself. "Shawn, you jerk, why did you say you'd play for Teresa?" Crystal mumbled. Her lack of concentration allowed Caleb just to trot through the pattern.

It was dark when they headed outside to the trailers. Crystal went over to see Shawn. "What song is it that you and Teresa are doing for the assembly Friday?" she asked.

"Uh, it's suppose to be a surprise." Shawn grinned.

"A surprise? What do you mean, a surprise?"

"I just can't tell you; it would ruin the effect." He sounded serious.

"How would two broken arms on the guitar player affect the tune?" Crystal threatened.

"Come on, we've been over this before, right?"

"I guess, but . . . well . . . I never, it's just. . . . It's just that I'm not sure of why I feel this way," Crystal blurted out.

"Hey, maybe we need to talk sometime; I'm not too sure of my feelings, either. I mean, this is all kind of new to me, and I don't think I'm doing too good of a job."

"Tonight?" she asked.

"Well, I've got to go . . . I'm kind of busy. We'll find some time this week. Say, tomorrow night after practice I want to come over and try to get that safe open. I think I know a way to do it. Are your folks complaining about it being in the front yard?"

"Not really. But Mom says if it's not gone by the first of the month she's going to sell it to the highest bidder." Crystal's mind bounced off her feelings for Shawn and back to the safe in her yard.

That evening she took some time to carefully reread the account of the mill closure at Winchester. It wasn't very interesting—mainly facts, figures, and accusations. There were lists of how many board feet of lumber were cut every year from 1902 to 1962. There were lists of plant supervisors, the biggest tree cut, and how many railroad cars of lumber went out during World Wars I and II.

Karla bounced down the stairs to Crystal's bedroom. "Crys—it's the telephone. Dad says you should come talk to the newspaper."

"Newspaper? Maybe it's about being one of the team captains?" Crystal hustled up the stairs.

"Wow, listen to this!" Crystal said, hanging up the phone. "The Lewiston reporter is going to be out tomorrow afternoon for a photo of that old safe. He wants Shawn, Betsy Jo, Gabrielle, and me to pose by it. Wild, huh?"

"What's the big deal?" Karla asked.

"Oh, they want to do a feature called 'Memories of a Milltown' or something like that. What am I going to wear? I wish I could do something with my hair. Maybe I'll wear that green western blouse. Oh, I guess it doesn't matter in black and white. Anyway, I've got to call the others— but Shawn isn't home. Why isn't Shawn home and what does he want to talk to me about?

"Karla, did I tell you Shawn wants to have this big serious discussion with me? Have you ever had a serious discussion with a boy? Sure you have, with Michael, right? Anyway, I'll call Betsy Jo and Gabrielle; I'll ask them what they are wearing." Crystal ran down the stairs. "I'll use the office phone!" she hollered as she shut the door behind her.

It took two calls to Betsy Jo and three to Gabrielle to decide what to wear. The three girls finally realized that it was so cold outside all anyone would see was their coats, but they did agree on green wool scarves around their necks.

Crystal started to call Shawn about eight. *Surely he's home now,* she thought. But then she waited. She didn't want to seem pushy, and she was afraid of finding out where he was. At 9:00, it was time to call. But she hesitated. "I'll die if you aren't there," she moaned to herself. "I've got to call, even if I just leave a message. He needs to know about the picture."

She dialed his number, and hung up on the last number. "Crystal LuAnne Blake," she lectured herself, "this is ridiculous behavior." She dialed again.

"Sorensens'." The voice belonged to Shawn's dad.

"Uh, Mr. Sorensen, this is Crystal. . . . Is Shawn . . . could you take a message for Shawn, I mean if he's not home?"

"He's been home all evening, Crystal. He's down in the family room; let me get him for you."

"Hi, Crys. What's up?" Shawn sounded cheerful.

"Oh, hey . . . I thought you said you were going to be gone tonight."

"Gone? No, I don't think I said that. Anyway, here I am. What's happening?"

"I got a call from the Lewiston paper, and they want to do a feature on the closing of the mill. And they heard about the safe, so they want a picture of all us with it, tomorrow after school."

"Wow, our picture, huh? Sort of Butch Sorensen and the Sunshine Girls. . . . What do you think of that?"

"I was thinking of 'Lil' Flash Strikes Again,' " she laughed.

"OK, I'll see you at school tomorrow."

"Yeah, sure. Are you sure you didn't say you

were going somewhere tonight?"

Shawn sighed. "I said I was tied up tonight, but that doesn't mean I have to go somewhere."

Then it dawned on Crystal that Shawn could have company. *That's it. He has someone there.*

"Teresa?" Crystal almost shouted it out. "Teresa? Is Teresa there?"

"Sure," Shawn responded, "do you need to talk to her?"

There was a long pause on the phone.

"Crys, did you need to speak to Teresa?"

"You've got to be kidding. See you tomorrow." She hung up the phone.

"What is she doing over there this late at night? What's this about being down in the family room?" Crystal muttered as she entered the bathroom to brush her teeth.

"Teresa Patterson, you're living on thin ice," she said to the mirror, "very, very thin ice."

5
A POPULAR ATTRACTION

D RESSING FOR HIGH SCHOOL IN WINCHESTER, Idaho, differed greatly from southern California. November in California was still the last dregs of summer. Hot east winds blowing across the valley, and tans had not yet faded.

Now Crystal dressed not to please anyone in particular, but to stay warm. It would be unheard of not to wear jeans and sweaters and coats. Pullover knit hats were quite acceptable as well.

During a class break Crystal had her first chance to visit with Shawn. Just as she walked up, Teresa and Dusty stopped to chat, too.

"Dusty, you ought to see Shawn's silver belt buckle collection. You'd think he was a regular Larry Mahan. Isn't it something, Crystal?" she smiled her upturned-nose, I'm-a-happy-little-rich-girl smile.

"Teresa, I need to talk to Shawn, do you mind?" Crystal sounded snappier than she wanted.

"No sweat." Teresa smiled again. "We were headed down to get an apple. You want an apple? It beats taking a bite out of me."

They moved on down the crowded hall leaving

Crystal and Shawn. "Well, Miss Congeniality, what can I do for you?" Shawn leaned against his locker. "Okay," he sighed, "I showed Teresa my buckle collection. She's been into rodeo for a long time so I thought she'd like to see it.

"Now, what you are wondering is what's Teresa Patterson doing over at my house last night. Well, we were practicing our duet for the assembly Friday. No, I can't tell you about it, because the is supposed to be full of surprises. You'll just have to trust me. You will have to trust me, 'cause you're my best friend," he added in a softer tone.

"I am?" Crystal stammered.

"Besides, Teresa's not my type," he admitted.

"What type is she?"

"You know, pushy, jealous, possessive." He grinned.

Crystal blushed. "And what type am I?"

"Why, you are pushy, jealous, possessive, and blonde," he laughed. "That's my type!"

"Hey, I'm sorry I was . . ." Crystal started.

"Less than perfect?" Shawn prompted. "Listen, I'll let you be less than perfect, if you allow me to be, too. As long as we try not to make a habit of it, right?"

"Yeah, well, really, I'm sorry for sounding so . . . so. . . ." Crystal stopped.

"Hey, there's the bell. See you at noon, and— why don't you tell Teresa you're sorry?" Shawn shot off down the hall.

She watched him head into the biology lab, and then turned to go into Mrs. Brady's English class. She spotted Teresa and Shawn's words came to mind.

"Tell Teresa," he had said. Crystal felt foolish enough with Shawn, but knew she couldn't talk to Teresa. Teresa Patterson was one of those girls that you had to maintain equality with at all times. As long as you proved yourself as strong and competent as she was, then you could be her friend. But if you showed one sign of weakness . . . if ever you let your hair down, admitted to failing, then she would be your worse enemy, so Crystal thought.

She sat down and pulled out her homework assignment. The class plodded along through the hour, but she didn't pay too much attention. All the time a debate raged in her mind about talking to Teresa: "I've got to! I can't!" Crystal wished she could be like Gabrielle who never seemed to care what others thought. She could always speak her mind and be herself.

Fourth period was just about like third. Crystal's internal debate raged on. She hardly spoke to Gabrielle as they waited in line for lunch. She sat playing with her "Surprise Stew" when Gabrielle interrupted her thoughts.

"OK, Crys, where are you at? You've done figure eights in your stew for ten minutes. Either eat it or talk. This is ridiculous." Her dark-haired friend spoke with concern.

"Oh," Crystal sighed, "I don't know. I mean, Gabrielle, how can you always be so confident of yourself? You know, you just blurt out what you feel. You're not worried what others think; you're just yourself. But me, well, I'm always trying to maintain some supergirl image, and I can't do it. Really, it's just a little thing. But I've been kind of . . . well, kind of hostile toward Teresa lately. No big deal. But I don't like being that way, so I ought to apologize. But I can't. I'm so afraid of losing status, or something. How can you always be in control? I admire you for it."

Gabrielle just sat there. Crystal looked up and realized that there were tears coming to Gabrielle's eyes. She stared down at the table and didn't speak.

"Did I say something? Gabrielle, what's wrong?" Crystal whispered.

"Let's go somewhere." Gabrielle stood and picked up her lunch plate. Crystal followed. It was cold, but they bundled up and went outside and sat on the steps in front of the gym.

Gabrielle looked out at the mountains in the distance. "So the California Lil' Flash thinks I have it all together. That's really funny. I've spent fourteen years trying desperately to like myself. I was the little girl with the jet black hair and the dark skin who was always different than all the other girls. I mean there were the boys and the girls, and then there was little Gabrielle. She's Indian, you know.

"I was the only kid in kindergarten who was asked, 'Do you live in a teepee? Can you shoot a bow and arrow?' " Gabrielle sighed. "I actually got sent to the nurse's office once a month to get checked for lice in my hair. Do you have any idea what that does for self-esteem? No one else was ever sent to the nurse's office.

"A kid hears all the comments. 'Lazy Indians.' 'Our little Nez Perce.' 'Now, Gabrielle, don't go on the warpath.' Crystal, I've cried myself to sleep wishing I could be blonde and fair skinned like you are. Then I get really mad at others, and proud to be Nez Perce. I'm ready to take on the world. But the next minute some dude at a rodeo insinuates that Indian girls are fun to be with, but you wouldn't want to get serious with one.

"Winning the role as class cheerleader last September was the first time the class ever selected me for anything. So you sit there and wish you were like me? Crystal, you are one of the neatest girls I ever met. My suggestion is if you feel guilty about saying something to Teresa, then go get it straightened out right now. But don't try to compete with girls like her. She's a pro at keeping people in their place. You've got to be yourself."

Crystal rubbed her hands together and then warmed them by blowing on them. She took her scarf and wiped some tears off her cheeks and jammed her hands back into her pockets. She didn't look over at Gabrielle. Finally she spoke.

"Kind of silly, isn't it? I fuss and stew about miscommunication, and you get to live in prejudice. Sometimes I'm really stupid."

"Hey, listen. It's not all that bad. I mean, I don't want you to think it's all horrible. It's just that I've never really had a non-Indian friend that I could complain to. You know what I mean? Anyway, things have gotten better. Besides, I like being an Indian now. After all, it's common knowledge that Indian girls are more beautiful," she laughed.

"I won't argue that. There are two million girls in southern California who would trade ten years of their life to be as brown as you are." Crystal faltered, "Hey . . . can I apologize for the whole Anglo race?"

"Lil' Flash, you're one of the good ones. Tell you what, whenever you're riding across the prairie in a covered wagon and all of a sudden you find yourself surrounded by 20,000 vicious redmen, just say, "Hey, fellas, wait a minute. I'm a good buddy of Gabrielle Northstar.""

Crystal laughed, "And what will they say?"

"Oh, they'll say, 'Gabrielle who?' "

"Well. I'm going to apologize to Teresa because I'll feel guilty for a week if I don't, and I'm not going to give anyone the pleasure of making me feel guilty for a whole week."

The girls returned to the hallway. Crystal spotted Teresa sitting on the floor, leaning against the wall, doing some last-minute home-work.

"Teresa, listen, I'm sorry about being so . . . you know, kind of angry sounding this morning. Forgive me, huh?" Crystal stammered.

Teresa just looked up for a moment, then smiled. "Sure . . . I mean . . . uh, no big, really. You may not believe this, but I have my off days, too."

Crystal didn't know whether Teresa was teasing or being serious. Either way, Crystal was relieved to have been able to apologize.

The two afternoon classes flew by, and Crystal found herself riding home with Karla. "You know, Karla, I really think that I've got a chance at winning that cutting horse event. You ought to see how well Caleb does. Are you going to come to the rodeo in Pendleton?"

"I've got to work on my senior project. But I'm going to Spokane with you. Maybe you can introduce me to a cowboy."

Crystal laughed, "That would be a switch. 'Say, buddy, have you got an older brother for my sister?' " Both girls howled as they entered their driveway.

"The safe! I almost forgot about the pictures. They're going to be here at 3:30. I've got to hurry and take care of Caleb before they show up."

"Is he going to be in the picture?" Karla asked as they got out of the car and headed up the raised deck sidewalk.

"Yeah, why not? I think that he did as much as anyone."

Crystal hurried through the chores with Caleb and led him over to the front yard about the time that Gabrielle drove up. Shawn and Betsy Jo arrived just a few moments before the photographer. He wanted to take several photos. Then he took down all their names. He promised that it would be in the next day's paper.

Betsy Jo headed back to Nezperce, while the other three went to rodeo team practice.

Crystal and Gabrielle spent the afternoon riding the poles. Crystal was just learning the routine, but Gabrielle could really fly. As Crystal watched her Indian friend, she thought about Gabrielle's earlier comments. *She gains acceptance by being really good,* Crystal thought. *I wonder if she would have gotten elected cheerleader if she hadn't been so important to the rodeo team?*

Even after a good practice, Crystal realized that she would not fare too well in the pole bending event. It was just too new, and she was still too unsure of making that many turns. As she practiced she formulated her plan of attack for the Pendleton Rodeo. In the cutting horse event she would do her best to win. In barrel racing, her goal was to score her best time ever. And in pole bending she wanted not to make a fool of herself. She knew she wouldn't place, but she didn't want to be last either.

That evening Crystal was swamped with homework. While she was writing a book report, her mom called her to the phone. When she finally got off the line she went over to where Karla and Allyson were sitting on the couch and flopped down between them.

"Hey, that was the newspaper again. They like this story, so tomorrow they are going to pay for a locksmith to come up and unlock the safe. They'll send a photographer back for a first picture of the safe's contents. Isn't this exciting?"

"You're going to get your picture in the paper again?" Karla asked.

"He didn't mention us. It's just the old safe he wants. They must be hard up for news," Crystal shrugged.

The following afternoon, Crystal relaxed. There was rodeo practice only for the boys' riding events. That meant Shawn had to be over at the arena early. Betsy Jo was stuck with chores at home, so when the photographer and locksmith showed up, only Crystal and Gabrielle were there to greet them.

Hiram Owensby looked to Crystal just like a locksmith. He drove an old green pickup that was loaded down with toolboxes and odds and ends. Piles of printed instructions scattered throughout the cab of the vehicle. He wore small, gold-framed glasses and a leather cap with heavy, fur earflaps down and tied under his chin. He and the photographer approached the big black safe, and Mr. Owensby squatted down in front of it to inspect it up close.

"It's beautiful! This is one beautiful safe," the older man exclaimed.

Crystal walked around in front of it to see what the man was looking at. It looked just the same to her. A black metal box with four little eagle's-claw legs and a rusty-looking dial on the door.

"Ladies, you have yourself a real antique. A 1902 Walkermade Safe. In its day it was the top of the line. Safes like this one made some old boys give up robbing banks. It will clean up. With a little restoration, well, I'll give you $100 for it, and you can have whatever is inside."

"You're kidding." Gabrielle was expressionless.

The old man looked over at the two girls. He paused a moment, then spoke up. "OK. I'll give you $250, but I can't go any higher. Don't even try."

"Uh, Crystal?" Gabrielle mumbled.

"Well, maybe. I mean, that sounds good. But we won't let it out of our sight until you open it up, OK?"

"All right. Now, let a professional man get to work."

The girls sat down on the raised deck sidewalk and watched as Hiram Owensby put his years of experience into practice. He spun the dial over and over. Then he jiggled the handle repeatedly.

He took about ten minutes tapping the center of the dial with a small hammer. Finally he started sorting through the papers in his truck. He pulled out a small blue scroll, unrolled it, and slapped it down on the hood of his truck. "Girls, read the number on the plate on the back of that baby," he called.

"8994-32-1902, F, I think," Crystal responded.

"E or F? It makes a difference," Mr. Owensby called.

"It's too hard to tell," Crystal said.

"Well, let me look because it makes all the difference in the world." Mr. Owensby leaned over. "You're right, it's too hard to read."

"What's the difference?" Crystal asked.

"If it's an F, there's no problem. Just a few spins and taps and I'll have it open."

"And if it's an E?" Crystal wondered where this was leading.

"If that baby's an E, I'll up my price to $500. They only made about 100 of those models. They were too impractical. They cost about three times more than a regular safe. Old man Walker made those 100 himself. He had a patented lock that no one has ever duplicated. No one can pick them or open them without the combination. He figured that it would revolutionize the safe business."

"Sounds great to me. What went wrong? Didn't they work?" Gabrielle asked.

"They worked all right. They worked too good.

If you ever lost the combination there was absolutely no way anyone in the world could get inside. Walker set the combinations, sent the numbers with the safe, and refused to write them down anywhere else. Well, everybody can lose a piece of paper, and most of the folks were stuck with a big black box that they couldn't open. It was just too good."

"You mean, you can't open it?" Crystal sounded surprised.

"Only if it's an E," he said. "If it's a F, then this gismo should solve the problem." He pulled out a small, gray metal box with several wires drooping from it. "Imagine, a Walkermade E! Incredible!" he mumbled.

"Silent tumblers, that's what old man Walker invented. Not even our computer age has figured out how to hear them. Well, here goes." The old man licked a couple of suction cups attached to the end of the wires. Then he flipped several switches on the box and started turning the dial on the safe. After a couple minutes he stood up and looked at the girls.

"Well, I'll be. The first one I've ever seen. It is a Walkermade E. Just as quiet as a cat in a doghouse."

"You mean you can't open it?" the photographer from the paper asked.

"No one on earth can. Unless you had the combination. Since there are thousands or millions of possibilities of combinations, only a wild guess would actually hit the right one."

"We'll never open it? That's incredible," Crystal moaned.

"Well," the old locksmith said, starting to pick up his tools, "you might write the Snake River Lumber Company and find out if they have any old records of the combination. Or you could take some educated guesses. You see, Walker-made E's were so notorious for not being able to get into, that often folks would have Walker set the combination to some important number they could remember . . . like a birthday, or anniversary, or something. Anyway, my offer holds whether you open it or not—$500. I'll even come up here and pick it up," he stated.

"Uh, sure, we'll, er, talk about it and get back to you, Mr. Owensby." Crystal was trying to sort it all out in her mind.

She and Gabrielle mused as the photographer and locksmith drove down the hill. "We can't contact Snake River Lumber. If by any chance there was information in there about the mill closure, they for sure wouldn't want us to see inside," Crystal commented.

"So we either sell it and forget the whole mystery," Gabrielle suggested.

"Or we try to find a number or date or something." Crystal pointed at the safe as she talked.

"Hey, didn't you tell me that one book had facts and figures on the lumber mill?" Gabrielle sounded excited.

"Yeah, it does! Do you suppose there is a clue in all those statistics?"

"What can we lose?" Gabrielle suggested.

Crystal threw her arm around Gabrielle. "Right, and we can always sell it to Mr. Owensby. That $500 would buy some new rodeo team shirts, or something like that."

Crystal was excited to see the paper with all of their pictures in it. It made page one of the "Country Features" section. She thought the picture made her look a little chubby. But maybe it was just that jacket, she rationalized.

That night she hurried through chores and homework so she could reread the book about the economy of northern Idaho. She wrote down every six-digit combination of numbers she could find.

When she got through, it was almost midnight. But she found forty-seven possibilities. "And maybe none of them work," she moaned. Two numbers especially attracted her. The first day that the mill was in production was October 23, 1902. So Crystal deduced 10-23-02 as a possibility. Also, there was a legal description of the property that the company owned as sections 17 and 18 of township 11. Perhaps it could be 17-18-11.

Crystal ran up the stairs to ask her dad to come out with her and try the numbers. When she got up into the dark living room she realized that everyone was already in bed and the house was shut up for the night. She could see a few flickering shadows—reflections peeking out the air vent of the wood stove.

Just as well, she thought. *It's too cold out there anyway.* She started to the kitchen to turn on a light when she saw a movement out on the front lawn.

"Maybe it's a deer." She tiptoed to the window. She didn't want to turn on the sidewalk lights because that might scare the animal away. As she peered outside and adjusted her eyes, she recognized human forms out by the safe. A flashlight beam seemed to reveal them attempting to pick it up.

Instinctively Crystal flipped on the sidewalk lights and ran out the door. "Hey! What are you guys doing?"

She startled three very large men. They turned toward her. All of sudden she felt very, very alone.

6
THE DIRECT APPROACH

DADDY!" CRYSTAL YELLED WITHOUT TAKING HER eyes off the men. She tried to remember whether she had shut the door or left it open. "Daddy!"

A man in a dark wool hat started up the yard toward Crystal.

"Daddy?"

"Right here, princess." Suddenly, Mr. Blake stood beside her. He held a double-barreled shotgun across his arm. "I presume you fellas intend to get out of here before the deputy sheriff shows up or this crazy old double barrel accidently goes off in your direction."

Mr. Blake pointed his gun in the general direction of the safe.

"Gary, come on!" one of the others called as the men scampered into a dark-colored pickup and tore off into the night.

"You all right, kiddo?" Mr. Blake called out.

"Yeah, I'm sure glad you're a light sleeper." Crystal turned to see her mother at the door.

"Matthew, what did those guys want?"

Mr. Blake escorted Crystal back into the living room. "Well, honey, I guess they wanted the kids' safe out there. Why don't you make us some hot chocolate, and let's sit down and talk about this. Crystal, I think maybe we've been too busy to understand what's going on. Fill me in again. What's this safe business really about?"

For the next hour Crystal sat with her mom and dad talking about all she had learned about the closing of the mill.

Catherine Blake was the first to respond, "Well, I guess they could have wanted the safe as an antique. Mr. Owensby told you it was worth at least $500."

"True," Crystal's dad added, "but no one but some old locksmith like Hiram Owensby would know what it's worth. I figure somebody's wanting the contents."

"Were they trying to open it, or pick it up?" Mr. Blake inquired.

"Oh, I'm sure they were trying to pick it up." Crystal added, "Dad, were you really going to use the shotgun?"

"Honey, I didn't have time to unlock the shells. It was unloaded."

"You were sure taking a chance."

"I suppose, but I didn't have time to think about it. Anyway, if they were trying to pick it up, then they didn't know the combination."

"I thought no one could know the combination."

"Except the Snake River Lumber Company. Somebody there might," Mr. Blake added.

"So it probably wasn't them," Crystal's mom concluded.

"Unless . . . unless there is something in there they wanted, and they didn't have the combination. Crystal said if there were papers to prove the mill was just a tax dodge, then they owed the workers some sort of severance compensation . . . plus some legal fines. They might even have to pay twenty-five years' interest on the money."

"What are we going to do?" Crystal asked.

"Well, tomorrow I'm going over to the courthouse at Nezperce and talk to the sheriff. I don't like shadowy fellows on the front yard every night," Mr. Blake said.

"What about tonight? I mean, what if they come back?" Crystal pointed out.

"I don't think they will be back. We'll leave on the light outside and in the living room. They won't want to get within shotgun range. Anyway, kiddo, let's face it. All the mystery in the world isn't worth anyone getting hurt. If they want it bad enough, they can have it. Right?"

"Yeah . . . well. Sure, you're right. But still. . . ." Crystal wondered aloud.

"Bedtime, Lil' Flash," Mrs. Blake laughed.

"Lil' Flash! How did you know about that name?"

"A mother knows a lot more than you realize."

"And that, young lady, is the gospel truth," her dad chuckled. "Now, let's have some prayer and let the Lord take care of this."

That night as Crystal lay in bed she tried to figure out the mystery of the safe. *I never even told Mom and Dad about finding some possible combinations. I'm sure glad to have parents who stop and listen . . . and pray.* Crystal felt very secure as she drifted off to sleep.

Crystal was late getting up and had to rush to ride with Karla to Highland High. She had wanted to try out some of the combinations, but there was no time.

The morning flew by as she repeated the previous night's events, first to Gabrielle and then to Shawn. "I've got to get home and try those combinations," she moaned.

"Hey, it's Thursday. Remember, we've got roping and cutting practice. We've got to get over there early," Shawn reminded her.

"Oh, yes. Well," Crystal sighed, "let's try them tonight. I guess we could use a flashlight, right?"

"Yeah, if our fingers don't freeze," Shawn frowned. "Hey, now don't get mad, but I've got to practice for the assembly tonight."

"Me? Me get mad?" Crystal faked indifference. "If you get closer to her than two feet, I'll feed you both to the sharks."

"Oh, well, as long as it's nothing serious," Shawn laughed.

After school Crystal planned to trailer Caleb and then try a couple of the safe combinations before rodeo practice. She and Karla were half way up the drive when Crystal noticed something different.

"It's gone! They stole it! It's gone. Look, the safe is gone." She jumped out of the car and ran over to the former site of the safe, now marked only by indentations in the grass and snow. "Maybe Mom and Dad know something." Crystal scurried up to the house and through the living room shouting, "Dad! Mom? Dad?"

"Hey, speedy, look. Here's a note." Karla picked up a paper on the room divider near the door. Crystal grabbed it out of Karla's hand and read out loud:

"Gone to Lewiston; we've got Allyson. We'll be home by six. Preheat the oven to 350°, and we'll bring home a you-bake-it pizza."

"Great. Just great. They take off, and someone steals our prize."

"Well, the lawn does look nicer," Karla commented as she scooted up the stairs."

"I've got to call the sheriff. There's been a robbery," Crystal called after her.

Karla stuck her head out of the bathroom. "I don't know, Crystal. How about waiting until Dad gets home? It could be he knows something about all this."

"Well, I know all about it. Those men stole my safe. You weren't out there last night. Those guys were serious. They probably hung out until everyone left, then whamo!" Crystal announced.

"Still, I think you should wait. Let Dad handle all that. He's got some good friends to contact. He even mentioned about going over to Nez-perce this morning, remember?"

Crystal flung herself down in a chair. "Oh, I guess I could wait. But they stole it. I know they did."

Once again Crystal gave herself to the daily routine of combing and brushing Caleb. Now in November, his coat was getting long and his mane shaggy. Crystal wanted to trim him, but knew he needed the warmth for the winter. By the time she led him over to the front of the house, Gabrielle greeted them.

During the trip over to Pattersons' arena, the girls debated the whereabouts of the missing safe. But once the girls entered the arena, their thoughts turned toward rodeo. In just two days they would travel to Pendleton to face one of the toughest high school teams in the country. Crystal began to feel the pressure.

At first she and the others just watched from the sidelines as the team ropers practiced. Once in a while she would help round up and bring back a calf that got away. At cutting time she proudly led her teammates out into the center of the arena. Crystal knew it was her turn to shine. In all the other events she practiced, Crystal was constantly trying to impress her teammates and prove why she should have a place on the team. But with cutting it was different. They all knew why she was on the team, and she didn't need to impress anyone. So she always tried to pick the most difficult looking animal to cut out of the herd. She figured if she and Caleb could learn on the tough ones, all the others would be easy.

Caleb seemed delighted to have something to do besides run around poles and barrels. He would dash into the herd, bluff out the victim, and badger it right back out to the middle of the arena. The only problem she ever had with him was convincing him that the contest was over, that it was all right to let the animal return to the herd.

She had just completed her third practice run when Shawn rode out to Crystal.

"Hey, cowgirl, you've got a fan club waiting over there for you," he announced.

"Where? For me? Those guys? What do they want?"

"You're the famous Crystal Blake, aren't you? Go ask them."

"Yeah, well, if you aren't doing anything, why don't you ride over there with me?"

"You got it, Lil' Flash." He pulled alongside of her as they rode to the fence.

Crystal saw two men in business suits and overcoats leaning up against the fence talking to Mr. Duffy, the rodeo coach. They looked like ordinary city guys to Crystal. She tried to figure out if they were the guys in the shadow of her lawn the night before. She really couldn't tell.

Seeing them all dressed up made her realize how grubby she was.

She wore a faded pair of blue jeans and her oldest boots. Her western blouse had been new the first time she met Shawn, but by now it was starting to wear and fade. A jeans jacket and her brown beaver, felt cowboy hat completed the wardrobe. Her hands, face, and long, blonde hair were covered with the fine dust that hung in the air of the indoor arena.

Mr. Duffy nodded as the two rode up. "Well, fellas, I've got to do a little coaching. Like I said, maybe we could work something out when it comes time to print our yearbook. Now those two there," he said pointing to Crystal and Shawn, "they just moved to town this year, and they added just enough to make us real state contenders. Some years, things do go right in coaching." Mr. Duffy climbed over the fence and stepped to the center of the arena.

"I'm Crystal. Did you want to see me?" Instinctively Crystal took off her hat and slapped it against her leg, letting the dust fly off before replacing it.

"Sure do, young lady. And let me say you've got a great cutting horse. I know folks who'd give $3,000 for a horse like that." The older man of the two did the talking.

"Thanks. Caleb's not for sale, of course. He's got a lot more to teach me." Crystal flashed a polite smile.

"Well, yes. If you've got a minute to come on down we'd like to talk to you. Maybe there is a private spot around here where we could discuss a proposition that might be very beneficial to you and your team."

"Crystal likes talking from a saddle," Shawn interrupted.

"And who are you?" the man stared at Shawn as if trying to locate his name in a file.

"I'm Crystal's agent," he bowed, "but who are you two?"

"Oh, excuse me, I'm Milton Powers, vice-president, public relations for the Snake River Lumber Company. And this is my associate, Mr. Lavantte," the older man responded. "Shawn . . . yes, you were the young man in the picture."

"Picture?" Crystal asked.

"Yes, that's why we are here. We saw your picture with the safe in the Lewiston paper. As you know, the safe was ours before the mill tragically burned down and we sold the property to the state for a park. Technically, I suppose it is ours still. But the point is, I am in the process of putting together a display of the early days of the lumber business at our headquarters down in Boise, and it would be great to have that classic old safe fixed up and used in our display. So, I wondered if we could strike a deal to buy it from you?"

The man reminded Crystal a lot of Mr. Myers, her sixth-grade, prealgebra teacher. *I never did like Mr. Myers,* she thought. While she contemplated a response, Shawn spoke up.

"Well, now, an antique safe like that is probably worth a lot of money." He smiled as he pushed his hat back.

"Oh, I'm not sure it's an antique—not in a valuable sense, but it does represent an era in our company's business. I was talking to Mr. Duffy about some of the needs of your team, and I told him I thought we might just be able to swing new outfits for your whole team, a big ad in the yearly program, and of course a healthy bonus of, say—$100 each for the four of you who found the safe and dug it up."

"Well, that's a good start," Shawn responded. "I'll . . ."

"Actually, Mr. er . . ." Crystal tried to interject.

"Powers."

"Mr. Powers," Crystal shrugged, "someone st . . ."

Shawn immediately cut her off. "Crystal, wait. We need to consider this generous offer. We'll be right back." He motioned for Crystal to join him back in the middle of the arena.

"Shawn, the safe's stolen. We don't have anything to sell them anyway. Why lead them on?"

"Listen." Shawn rubbed the back of his neck and stared across the arena. "They're from Snake River Lumber Company, right?"

"We don't even know that for sure. Did they

show us a business card or anything?" Crystal questioned.

"You're right. They didn't. But suppose they really are from the lumber company. That means they didn't steal the safe, right? Then who did and why? Also, why do they want to buy the safe?" Shawn gestured back at the two men who still stood next to the fence.

"Right! Maybe we ought to find out what they know and how much they want the safe before we tell them it's gone." Crystal was beginning to understand.

"You got it. Let's see if we can get them to say anything else." They rode back to the two men.

"Well, what did you two decide?" Mr. Powers boomed.

"It seems to us a fine old safe like that might be worth a little more," Shawn suggested.

"More? Come on, kids. I already promised you an arm and a leg out of the company's generosity toward youth sports. I'm not here to haggle. We'll just have to get another safe," he threatened.

"You won't find another Walkermade E, will you, Mr. Powers?" Crystal added.

Mr. Powers stopped and turned. He nodded his head. "So you know about Model E's?"

"We know that there are only 100 on the face of the earth, if that many, and every locksmith in the country would like to have one and figure out how old man Walker built them. Yours isn't the first offer we've had," Crystal informed them.

"Well, well. A couple of professional business people here." Mr. Powers stuck his hands in his overcoat pockets. "Let's start this all over again. What's the asking price on the old safe?"

"Oh, I liked the new outfits for the team," Crystal grinned. "But we would need new hats, too."

"And," Shawn added, "four matching silver show saddles for the co-owners."

"What do you figure those saddles would cost?" Mr. Powers almost glowered.

"Fourteen fifty," Shawn countered.

"What—$1450? Look, kids . . ."

"A piece," Crystal added. "Four saddles, at $1450 each."

"Come on, Milton," the man named Lavantte suggested, "I told you this was not . . ."

"Just wait," Powers interrupted. "Now, I asked them what the going price was, and they told me. There's no harm in that." He turned back to the kids. "I figure I could suit up this team for $4,000 and another $6,000 buys the saddles. So you two are asking $10,000 for a safe that is only worth $1000 to $2000 on the antique market. Now, doesn't that appear a little bit high?"

"Sure, but you didn't count in the 'want-it' value," Shawn remarked.

"Want it?"

"Yeah, we got it, and you want it."

Mr. Powers looked out across the arena as if considering the alternatives. He took a big breath and sighed. "Well, let's talk a little more about this. I couldn't possibly spend $10,000 on a safe. That's our whole budget for the historical display. But if I could count some of this as public relations, I could split the sum and get by. Now, if you'll throw in a full-page ad in your yearbook, and a Snake River Lumber Company insignia on the cuff of your shirts?"

"Sorry, no commercial insignias are allowed in high school rodeo," Shawn told him.

"I'm sure we could get the ad," Crystal suggested. "But, we do have one problem. How do we know you are really from Snake River Lumber Company?"

"Boy, you two have been watching lots of detective shows on television." Mr. Powers reached into his pocket and brought out an engraved business card. He handed one to Shawn and one to Crystal.

"Well, we need to be careful." Crystal sat straight on Caleb looking down at the men. "Last night some guys tried to steal the safe right off my front lawn. Can you imagine that?"

"You don't say." Mr. Powers seemed genuinely surprised. "Did you find out who they were?"

"No, it was too dark to recognize them," she reported. "But I figure the safe must be worth a lot to somebody."

"When do we get the gear, I mean, provided we agree to your price?" Shawn asked.

"I still have to clear it with headquarters, you understand," Mr. Powers insisted. "I would imagine sometime in the next eight to ten weeks."

"Of course, we would need to pick up the safe right away. We need the display finished by the first of the month," Mr. Lavantte spoke up.

"Whoa!" Shawn waved his hand. "Let's put it this way, no money, no safe."

"Right," Crystal said. "We would need the $4,000 deposited on account down at Dartmouth's in Lewiston for the outfits. And the $6,000 left with Mr. Howard at The Western Saddlery for the saddles. Then we could let you have the safe."

"Now look. You two are trying my patience. I've tried to make a good deal for you, but you're asking for something impossible," Mr. Powers fumed.

"In that case, gentlemen, I think we'd better get back to practice." Shawn nodded to Crystal.

"Wait—oh, look . . . I was young once. . . . I know how frustrating waiting can be. I'll see what I can do," Powers said. "I don't want to spend all month up here. If I get the money deposited in those accounts by noon tomorrow, then we'll pick up the safe in the afternoon. Have we got a deal?"

"If we can find it by then," Crystal calmly

muttered as she took off her hat and shook the dust off her blonde hair.

"Find it!" Lavantte and Powers both shouted.

"What do you mean, find it?" Mr. Powers huffed. "It's right there in your front yard!"

"He means, we saw the picture in the paper and assumed . . ."

"Well, it's not there now," Crystal announced.

"But you said those guys last night failed." Powers's face burned crimson red.

"Oh, they did," Crystal assured him. "But they must have come back while we were all gone today, because it's nowhere in sight."

"You don't have it? You really don't have the safe?" Powers shouted.

"Don't have it, and don't know where it is." Crystal shrugged.

"But what's all this—this—conversation about price!" he screamed.

"Just wanted to see how serious you were," Shawn smiled.

"Yeah, we just wanted to know what we missed." Crystal looked down at two extremely angry men. "Been nice talking to you; give our best to Snake River Lumber Company."

Mr. Powers turned to his associate, "Let's get out of here, Gary. You just can't deal with kids."

The men stormed out of the arena while Crystal turned to Shawn. "Did you hear Mr. Powers call that man 'Gary'?"

100

7

FULL OF SURPRISES

CRYSTAL SHOOK HER HEAD, STOOD UP IN THE stirrups, and repeated, "Did he say 'Gary'?"

"Yeah, sure. So what? What's this all about?" Shawn leaned his left hand on the back of his horse and waited for Crystal's reply.

"Gary! That was the name of one of the men who tried to steal the safe last night. Someone started toward me, and the other said, 'Come on, Gary, let's go.'"

"Was it the same guy?" Shawn eased back down in the saddle and rode closer to Crystal.

"I couldn't tell. I mean, I didn't see any faces last night," she admitted.

"It doesn't make sense that that was the same guy. I mean, if those guys last night came back today and steal the safe, then they wouldn't show up wanting to buy it. I don't think Snake River Lumber stole the safe, but they sure wanted to buy it."

"And, man, they wanted to buy it. I was ready to sell it, if we only knew where it was," Crystal laughed.

"Not without seeing what's on the inside. I mean what if there was some cash in there? Or what if something even more valuable . . . what

if it had those papers about the mill shutdown?"
Shawn slapped his horse on the rump.

Crystal and Shawn rode over to the gates
where the team was about ready to practice
steer wrestling. "You know, Shawn, I'm kind of
glad that the safe is gone. Now I can just concentrate on Saturday's competition."

"Yeah, and I can concentrate on tomorrow's
assembly," he winked.

Crystal summoned every ounce of frown she
could muster and gave Shawn her best "you
turkey" look.

"Hey—just kidding. Listen, why don't you
haze for me, and I'll try throwing one of these
critters." Shawn quickly changed the subject.

"Really, you want me to haze for you?" Crystal's face brightened.

"Sure, you and Caleb should be naturals.
Don't know why I didn't think of it before. Come
on, you and Caleb ride along the right side of the
steer. Keep him in a straight line across the
arena until I jump him. Then while I'm throwing him, you can retrieve my horse."

Crystal lined up on the right side of the chute,
with Shawn back in the box. The gate opened,
the ring fell, the barrier broke, and she and
Caleb dashed off alongside the thundering steer.
Shawn rode up even with the steer, leaped down
on its back and threw it to the ground.

"All right!" Crystal yelled. "Nice work,
cowboy."

"Hey, I've got a new hazer," Shawn called. "How about it?"

Crystal and Shawn talked rodeo as they led the horses outside and got ready to leave. It was only two days away from the big event at Pendleton, and Crystal was starting to get worried. "Do I still look like such a novice?" she asked.

"You're really getting better and better every day, Crys. Remember what Gretchen told you? You and that horse really fit each other. I'll bet when we get busy in the spring, everyone will assume you've been going to Cheyenne every year."

"Cheyenne?" she blurted.

"Oh, you know, the big rodeo over there. The Frontier Days. 'Going to Cheyenne' is sort of a saying that means you're old-time rodeo folk. Anyway, don't get too nervous. You're going to do just fine. Don't go out and buy a new bit, though," he kidded.

Crystal threw her saddle blanket over his head. "Shawn, aren't you ever going to let me live that down?"

"Nope," he smirked.

At that moment Gabrielle breezed up and began loading her horse. "I heard we might get someone to buy our new outfits," she pumped Crystal.

"Uh, well, not unless we can find that safe."

"That's what I was afraid of. Anyway, we wouldn't have it before tomorrow. Remember

103

we're going down with Mrs. Patterson to pick out some new shirts."

"See you ladies tomorrow," Shawn called.

The short drive back to Winchester was even shorter as Crystal filled Gabrielle in on how badly the Snake River Lumber Company men wanted to buy the safe. As she unloaded Caleb in the corral, Crystal pushed her hat back. "Why don't you come over tonight and we'll work on that English homework. Are you any good at diagraming sentences?"

"There's never been a hoss I couldn't ride, nor a sentence I couldn't diagram," Gabrielle said in her deepest-voiced, western-movie-star imitation.

As Crystal headed back to the house, after Gabrielle left, she heard the roar of her parents' car. She flew around the west side of the house, between the pine trees, and out toward the driveway.

"Mom—Dad—hey, they stole it and we've got to call the police. I mean, I came home from school and it was gone. Without a trace. Then these guys from Snake River Lumber showed up at practice and tried to buy it off me for $10,000 and, boy, were they surprised when I told them that somebody stole it. You've got to call the sheriff. Did you go see the sheriff? Hi, Allyson, did you get a surprise in town? Well, what do you think, Dad?" Crystal stopped for breath.

Mr. Blake hugged Crystal as they hiked up the

deck sidewalk toward the front door. "Whoa, time-out, princess. Let's back up. Catherine, you'd better tell Crystal about the safe."

Mrs. Blake smiled. "Well, young lady, I really didn't like the looks of that ugly thing in the front yard. So I got Homer, who works for the city, to come down here this morning with a forklift and haul that thing around back. He put it in the toolshed. It just barely fit. So if you got a legitimate offer of $10,000, I suggest you call them up and take it."

"In the toolshed? The safe? Really?" Crystal jumped on the front porch. Allyson followed suit, skipping around behind her.

Then Crystal ran through the house shouting at a bewildered Karla, "It's in the toolshed. Mom put it in the toolshed!"

"Shut the back door!" Mrs. Blake called, but Crystal was outside in the toolshed before she finished the sentence.

She flew back inside the house slamming the door and heading for the stairs. "I've got to call Gabrielle and Shawn."

"Hold it, Crystal LuAnne." Mrs. Blake grabbed her shoulder. "You know better than to call friends during suppertime. Besides it's your turn to set the table."

"But, Mother! This is important!"

"So is building grace, charm, and responsibility in my daughter." Mrs. Blake turned Crystal around and headed her for the kitchen sink. "Go wash the rodeo off your hands and help me make a salad to go with this pizza."

Crystal sighed as she obeyed her mother. She peeked in the mirror at the dusty face and hair. "Grace and charm? Grace and charm . . . it sounds like the Kimberly twins." Crystal thought of neighbors they had when she was in kindergarten. She stuck out her tongue at the mirror. "That's for the Kimberly twins," she laughed.

During dinner Crystal explained how the two men wanted the safe and that one was named Gary. "What do you think, Dad, could it have been the same guy as last night?"

"I suppose. This whole thing is getting complicated. Maybe your mother is right. Call Snake River. See if you can get some gear for the team. I'm not sure you need another saddle. You've already got two, and you only have one horse."

"Mom, can I go call Gabrielle now? And can she come over and do homework? We need to work on some English."

"Sure. But remember tonight's the senior class meeting with their parents. Karla will be with us, so you and Gabrielle will have to baby-sit Allyson. Can you handle that?"

"No sweat. Two of us and only one three-year-old."

"I know it's lopsided," Mr. Blake laughed, "But we hope you can handle it even if you are outnumbered."

"Don't worry. Gabrielle's a good roper," Crystal giggled and reached for the phone.

Gabrielle was just walking up the sidewalk as Mr. and Mrs. Blake and Karla left for the meeting.

"Is it really out in your toolshed?" Gabrielle asked.

"Yeah, isn't that something? We had it all the time, and I didn't know it. Listen, I've got some numbers out of that old book. I want to try them all out on the safe," Crystal suggested.

"Sure. You have some light out there?" Gabrielle asked.

"Not really, but you could hold a flashlight, right? I mean, I really think I've got a winner in here if I can figure it out. Of course, it's kind of cold, too."

"Cold? Crystal, it's twenty-four degrees out there. Look! Look at your own thermometer." Gabrielle pointed to the kitchen window.

"And, since we're baby-sitting Allyson, we'll take her out there also. Come on. I'll get her suited up," Crystal decided.

Fifteen minutes later Gabrielle, Crystal, and Allyson squatted out in the Blake toolshed. Gabrielle held the flashlight, and Crystal tried to spin the old dial as she squinted at the numbers she had scribbled down the night before. Allyson played with whatever she could find in the deep recesses of the toolshed.

"Now," Crystal said, "do I spin this to the right or to the left?"

"Hah! You ask me?" Gabrielle laughed. "I've never even opened a gym locker. However, I did have a combination lock on a bike chain once."

"Which way did it turn?"

"Uh . . . to the right. Yeah, it turned to the right, twenty-four right, twenty-seven left, and twenty-five to the right," Gabrielle recited.

"How can you remember that?" Crystal questioned.

"Cause those were my measurements at the time." Then Gabrielle snickered. "I was a really fat little kid."

"You were fat? Really, you were fat?"

"A regular butterball, I used to live on my grandmother's Indian fry bread," Gabrielle admitted.

"What happened? How did you lose it?" Crystal asked.

"I started noticing boys, and they didn't start to notice me. So, off came the pounds. Of course, I had to give up fry bread."

"Well, I went to the right, then to the left, then back again. Nothing happened," Crystal reported. "Hold the light over here, and I'll try a different number."

"Did you call Shawn and Betsy Jo about the safe?"

"Yeah, but Betsy Jo's sick. No, that number didn't work. It's getting colder, isn't it?"

"Yeah, and Shawn—is he coming over?" Gabrielle flashed the light over Crystal's shoulder again.

"Oh, he's not at home. He went over to Teresa's to practice for tomorrow's assembly again." Crystal tried to sound casual.

"Over to Teresa's? Have you ever been over to Teresa's? Once they see that Patterson den, boys never come back the same. I was there for a birthday party. They invited the whole class."

"That one didn't work either. I'll try this one. What's so special about the Patterson den?" Crystal wasn't sure she wanted to know.

"Hey, did that work? No. I guess not. Anyway," Gabrielle continued, "Mr. Patterson must have won every rodeo in the west in his day. He's got silver and saddles and plaques and trophies that you wouldn't believe. Then on the walls he's mounted some of the big game he's shot. Anyway, all the guys thought they had died and gone to Texas, if you know what I mean."

"Well, I don't see what the big deal is for this song. I mean, just how much practice does it take?" Crystal asked.

"Does what take?" Garbielle laughed.

"A song. A song, you jerk!" Crystal poked at Gabrielle.

"You having any luck? I'm cold," Gabrielle shivered.

"Well, I'm on a roll. None of the numbers work, and I've got about a dozen more. Then I've got to go through all of them by turning to the left first."

"You'll what? Look, paleface, you've got one cold Indian here. Let's go get some hot chocolate and popcorn."

"Snake—snake!" Allyson came out from behind the safe hollering and swinging something green.

The girls screamed and clutched each other. Allyson was frightened by the girls' screams and started to cry. Finally they realized that she was swinging the end of a green garden hose and started to laugh.

"Come on, I'm tired, too. Let's go into the house," Crystal suggested.

She opened up the wood stove and tossed a couple more logs in. Then she helped Allyson out of her snowsuit, and all three girls went into the kitchen to fix some popcorn.

"Dad's probably right," Crystal said as she plopped down on the living room rug, waiting for the corn to pop. "We should just call up Mr. Powers in the morning and let him have it. Whatever is in there is locked up forever so it really doesn't matter who has the safe. Then we could have one great shopping spree tomorrow with that $4,000 credit."

Crystal made two big batches of buttered cheese popcorn while Gabrielle fixed the hot chocolate. They played color bingo with Allyson for about twenty minutes, and then Crystal carried her upstairs and tucked her into bed. When she returned, Gabrielle was working on her English homework.

"Remember this stuff?" she smiled.

"Oh, yeah, diagrams. What fun. Listen, this safe business, isn't it kind of dumb? I mean, why build a safe that nobody can get into? It doesn't make sense. And keeping the combination in your head, never writing it down. Who can remember a combination anyway?"

"I did," Gabrielle shrugged.

"Yeah, but that was different . . . you said it was your measurements. Was it really?" Crystal sat down at the kitchen table across from Gabrielle.

"I think so."

"Well, when you have some association like that, you remember. But what does a safe have to remember?"

"Maybe its measurements!" Gabrielle shouted.

"Yeah! I mean, they would always be the same, and if you forgot all you would have to do is get the yardstick. Dad's got a tape measure in the junk drawer. Come on, get the flashlight. Let's check it out."

Crystal and Gabrielle were in such a hurry that they left their coats inside. Gabrielle's teeth chattered as they huddled around the safe in the toolshed.

Crystal did the measuring. "Forty-one inches

111

by thirty-three inches by twenty-nine inches. That's 41-33-29. Let me try it."

She spun the dial a couple times to clear it. Her hand was shaking mostly from the cold as she twisted it around and stopped on the 41. Then she moved it slowly back past the 33 one whole rotation and stopped on the number. She took a deep breath, then twisted the old dial to the right once until the 29 came around. Crystal thought she heard the tumblers inside the lock fall into place.

"Grab that handle." Gabrielle was getting excited.

Crystal pulled the black handle down, but it didn't budge. "Maybe I missed lining the numbers up," she suggested.

"Hit that baby. Crank down on that handle, Crys."

Crystal stood up and pushed down on the handle with both hands, using her full weight.

Suddenly, decades of rust slipped away under the pressure and the handle swung down. "That's it! Gabrielle, that's it!"

"Open it! Open it!" she shouted.

"I can't. I mean the lock's open, but the door is sort of stuck. Maybe it's rusted. Where's Dad's crowbar?"

"Step aside, Lil' Flash. Let a woman do the job," Gabrielle laughed.

"OK, mountain momma, go to it." Crystal sounded anxious.

Gabrielle grabbed the handle, put her full weight against it, and yanked with all her might. Suddenly the safe door flew open. The force of the pull slammed Gabrielle back against Crystal who dropped the flashlight she'd been holding. Both girls tumbled against the door of the toolshed, screaming and yelling.

"It's open," Crystal yelled in the dark. "Get off me, Gabrielle. Where's the flashlight?"

"Off you? You're the one on me."

"Here's the light," Crystal called. "Look, you're on my legs."

"Well, what's that on me?" Gabrielle twisted her neck around to see behind her.

"Uh, well, it looks like a sack of . . . you know . . . steer manure," Crystal laughed. "Now get off me; let's see what's in there."

The girls scampered on their hands and knees towards the safe. "Gabrielle, look!" Crystal almost hissed.

Gabrielle shook her head in disbelief. "You've got to be kidding."

8

TEAM ROPING

I T'S EMPTY! THE SAFE IS EMPTY!" CRYSTAL
shouted.

Gabrielle grabbed the flashlight and pointed
it all around the toolshed. "Maybe something
fell out?"

The girls frantically searched around the safe,
then flopped down, leaning against each other's
back.

"It's sort of funny," Crystal sighed. "You
know, like the time Shawn, Betsy Jo, Brad, and I
went hunting for a gold mine and were about
100 years too late. Know what I mean?"

"So, the great mill fire mystery remains a
mystery," Gabrielle murmured as she pointed
the light toward the safe one more time. "It's a
cinch no one had been inside for many years.
That door jammed good."

"There's still a little mystery. Why did anyone
want to steal an empty safe?" Crystal was
puzzled.

"And why did that guy from Snake River
Lumber offer you all that stuff for it?" Gabrielle
added.

Crystal got to her feet. "Maybe he was legitimate. Anyway, he didn't ask to buy a safe with

114

anything in it. I'm going to call him up tomorrow and explain that we have the safe and see if the price still holds. New show saddles would be nice," Crystal announced as the two girls closed up the toolshed and raced back into the warm house.

Crystal dialed the phone to call Betsy Jo and Shawn while Gabrielle stirred some more hot chocolate. A half hour later Crystal finished the calls.

"What did they say?" Gabrielle sat on the living room rug and leaned against the couch.

"Well, Betsy Jo thinks she'll try to go to school tomorrow. Not that she is feeling any better, it's just that this boy's sort of taken an interest in her and she doesn't want to miss an opportunity to be asked out."

"No, no. I mean what did they say about the safe?" Gabrielle insisted.

"Oh, Betsy Jo said we should get as much as we can for the safe, but that if her one-quarter share went toward Highland High rodeo team gear, you'd have to let her win the barrel racing next time we compete against Nezperce."

"No chance," Gabrielle laughed. "How about Shawn. What did he say?"

"I called his house, but his mom said that he was still at Teresa's"

"Aha! Still at Teresa's! What did I tell you about Pattersons'?" Gabrielle pointed at Crystal as she talked.

"Hey, knock it off. Anyway I called Teresa's, and Shawn wasn't there. She said he had just left and that he was going to swing by here on his way home. So there!" Crystal flashed her prissiest, I-told-you-so smile. "Besides, Teresa said they mainly listened to some records. Something about the song at the assembly tomorrow."

"Records! Listened to records? That's worse, Crystal. Don't you know where Teresa's stereo is?" Gabrielle teased.

"I don't want to hear this," Crystal put her hands over her ears.

"Teresa's fabulous stereo is upstairs in her bedroom!" Gabrielle shouted.

Crystal yelled over the top of Gabrielle's voice, "I'm not listening to this. I can't hear a word you are saying."

"Her stereo is right there next to that pink, ruffled, four-poster bed with the white lace awning over the top." Gabrielle poured it on.

"I'm not listening!" Crystal yelled. Then she paused, and said, "Really, she has a pink, four poster with a canopy?"

"Yeah, that's true, but I made up the part about the stereo. It's down there in the den. Boy, you really got into that."

"You turkey. I ought to . . . I ought to . . . to tell Earl Roy Case that you want him to ask you to the Christmas party." Crystal faked a southern accent, "Earl Roy, honey, Miss Gabrielle is surely pining away to meet you. Why, it's your civic duty to ask her to the Christmas party before she dies of a broken heart." With that Crystal slipped off the chair laughing and rolled to the floor.

"You do that and the Battle of the Little Bighorn will look like a Sunday picnic in comparison," Gabrielle warned.

"What's the Little Bighorn?" Crystal asked.

"How come you palefaces always forget the battles we won? That was Custer's Last Stand, remember?"

A knock at the door startled them both. Crystal got up to answer it. "Hey, it's Shawn. He'll be surprised about the safe." Crystal hollered out as she approached the door, "Shawn—Shawn, the safe's empty." She opened the door. "It's—oh. Oh, no."

"Sorry to disappoint you, but I appreciate hearing news about the safe." The man was not smiling.

Crystal stammered, "Uh, Mr. Gary . . . I mean Mr. Lavantte, from Snake River Lumber."

"You have a good memory—unfortunately. Now, Miss Blake, the fellas and I have some business to discuss with you inside." He spoke harshly, in fast, choppy tones.

"Oh, I can't let you in. . . . I mean, you should come back when my dad's home, I mean no one's here but me and Gabr . . ." she looked around and didn't see Gabrielle at all. "Uh, me and my sister. But, my folks will be home any minute, and my . . . er, my ah, boyfriend, yeah, my boyfriend is on his way over. In fact, I thought that's who was at the door. . . . He'll be here and . . ."

Lavantte and two others walked into the living room pushing Crystal aside. All three wore heavy dark coats and gloves, but no hats.

"Let me get right to the point. I happened to be having dinner at the Inn, and I overheard someone say that he had used a forklift to move a safe from your lawn into your storage shed. Young lady, we want that safe, and we're going to take it with us." Lavantte looked the house over and walked into the kitchen. The back door was open just a bit. He opened it and looked out into the black night. Then he closed it and turned around to face Crystal who stood in the living room with her arms folded.

"Mr. Powers promised to put up some money. He said we would . . ."

"Quiet! I'm not Powers, and I'm not about to pay you anything. Now what was this you were shouting at the door? Did you say you opened the safe?"

"Yeah, and it's no big deal. It's empty."

"What?"

"You heard me," Crystal reported. "All you guys running around trying to get ahold of an empty safe. I don't get it."

"Where is it?" Lavantte ordered. "Young lady,

you had better be kidding." He grabbed her by the arm and hustled her towards the back door.

"Let me get my coat," she insisted.

He paid no attention as he pushed her out the back door. She thought about running, but the steel grip on her arm kept her in check.

"Where's the light?" Lavantte insisted.

"There's not one. I mean, the flashlight is inside." Crystal could feel her heart beating rapidly.

One of the men reentered the house and brought out the flashlight. All of the men shoved their way into the small toolshed. Lavantte never loosened his grip on Crystal's arm.

"She's right—it's empty," one of the men spoke up.

"It's empty now, but what if she already took the stuff out?" Lavantte suggested.

"No, really, it was empty. We, I mean, I was really disappointed. I thought maybe there would be some money or something, at least." Crystal was trying to stall until Shawn or her dad showed up.

"Young lady, you are in serious trouble. We intend to find whatever it was that was in the safe, even if we have to tear your house to shreds finding it. Now, there were some ordinary, bookkeeping-looking records that wouldn't mean a thing to anyone else. Give those to me right now. I'll let you keep the safe, and we'll be on our way. But, if you don't . . ."

Crystal bit her lip trying to imagine what was coming next.

"I'll put a bullet right through the head of that gray Appaloosa over in the pasture." He still didn't smile.

"Caleb! You can't do that! I told you the truth. It was empty. Really, it was empty! Why are you guys doing this?" Crystal cried.

"Clint, go get the horse," Mr. Lavantte motioned, and one of the men walked off into the dark toward the pasture and corral.

"Lord," Crystal prayed through her tears, "not Caleb . . . don't let them hurt Caleb."

"Look," she said to the men, "why would I lie to you? What would I possibly want with some old business papers? I mean, I thought maybe there was some cash inside the safe, but I swear it was empty. Why are you doing this?" Crystal was in tears.

"Hey, maybe she's telling the truth." The unnamed man with Lavantte spoke for the first time.

"Listen, Powers offered the kids up to $10,000 for this safe. No way did he want that hunk of metal. There had to be something in it. Where's Clint? Clint! Hurry up!"

Crystal could feel her tears starting to freeze on her face, and she shook in the northern Idaho night. "Maybe Caleb will break away," she told herself.

There was no reply to Lavantte's calling. He

turned to the other man, "Go find Clint. He probably got lost—and hurry!

"Young lady, you're holding papers that are invaluable to a person who knows how to use them. You don't seem to understand what I am willing to do in order to get them."

"But why is Snake River Lumber doing this? Where is your boss, Mr. Powers?" Crystal questioned.

"Powers doesn't know anything about this, but he will as soon as I get those papers. I guarantee he will." Lavantte stared out into the dark as if trying to spot his associates.

A noise and a shout from out in the pines between the house and the corral startled both Crystal and Lavantte.

"Barry? Barry! Did you find Clint?" Lavantte reached inside his coat and pulled out a gun. He waved it at Crystal, "Get in that toolshed!"

"I'm freezing! Let me go in the house," Crystal pleaded. But he threw her toward the safe. She tripped on something and fell to the cement floor. Lavantte started to close the door on her when she realized that she was sitting on the green garden hose that Allyson had played with earlier.

With her best panicked voice Crystal hollered, "Snake! It's a snake!"

Lavantte jumped back from the door when he saw the coiled object in the shadow of the tool-shed. As he did a rolled rope came crashing down on his hand, knocking the gun to the dirt. Instantly, another rope sailed over his head and shoulders and was jerked so tight that it lifted him off his feet and onto the frozen ground.

Crystal peered out to see Shawn jumping off Caleb, with the rope holding Lavantte dallied around the saddle horn and the big gray Appaloosa holding the line tight. Gabrielle stepped out of the night and into the light of the back porch holding a coiled rope. She reached down and picked up Lavantte's gun.

"Shawn! Gabrielle! Look out, there are two others out there!" Crystal warned.

"Yeah, but they are hog-tied," Gabrielle snorted. "Shawn got the first one, and I got the other."

"Where'd you come from anyway? I mean," Crystal smiled, "where did you go?"

"When those dudes showed up at the door I slipped out the back to go call for help. I ran around to the front just as Shawn drove up. We scurried to the back to find out what was happening and saw them push you outside."

Shawn continued, "Then when we were trying to figure out what to do, they started out in the dark, one at a time. So we mounted up Caleb and roped and tied them. We were worried when this guy pulled a gun. I mean, I didn't know they had guns. But anyway you took care of that."

"Yeah, well, it's a trick I learned from my

little sister. I'm freezing, let's go in," Crystal implored. "What do we do with them?"

Shawn gave the commands. "I'll hog-tie this main man. Gabrielle, you call the sheriff's office. There must be some charges to file against them."

The deputy sheriff was loading three very humiliated men into the back of his car when Mr. and Mrs. Blake and Karla pulled up.

"Crystal! What's going on here?" her dad gasped.

"Well, those guys came back for the safe, and, we . . . I mean, Shawn and Gabrielle and . . . me. We wouldn't let them have it."

Mr. Blake spent the next half hour listening to the full account about the empty safe and the late-night visitors. Mrs. Blake checked on Allyson who had slept through the whole ordeal and was really mad for having been waked up in the middle of the night.

When they finished telling about the events of the evening, Gabrielle and Shawn headed home. Mr. Blake called the Lewis County sheriff. Crystal waited up until the conversation was over.

"What did the sheriff say?" she asked.

He's going down to the jail and interrogate the guys tonight. But he thought it sounded like they were working on their own to get the safe and blackmail their own company out of some money. They just didn't figure the safe was empty."

Crystal stood close to the wood stove, with her back to the heat. "How about Mr. Powers? Where does he fit in?"

"Well, the sheriff doesn't know, but wants you to go ahead first thing and sell the safe to Powers. He figures if something is fishy, that will help force his hand. He said sell the safe, enjoy the profits, and leave the rest to him."

Crystal screwed up her face. "It's sort of strange . . . all this excitement about an empty safe." She looked at her dad.

"Yes, and the sooner we get it out of here," Mrs. Blake joined in the conversation, "the better I'll like it. It's been a real pain. Come on, Crys, time for bed. You've got a big day tomorrow."

Crystal was staring blurry eyed into her closet when her mom called her to breakfast. She quickly tossed on her robe and scrambled up the stairs.

"Mom, have you seen my blue ski sweater?" she asked.

"Karla's wearing her gray and pink one. Why don't you wear yours that is just like it?" Mrs. Blake suggested.

"I don't want to dress just like Karla. Why, people would say, you know." Crystal squirmed.

"They might say you were sisters. How horrible," Mrs. Blake smiled.

Karla arrived at breakfast all dressed and

ready for school. Crystal guessed that she'd made her bed and picked up her clothes, too. She was wearing the gray sweater with the row of pink hearts.

"See, Mom, that's why I can't wear the sweater. Look at Karla."

Mrs. Blake turned to look at Karla and then back at Crystal for an explanation.

"I mean, she looks great. Everybody goes 'Wow!' when she walks into the room with something new on. But me . . . I'm just the rerun. Sort of plain."

"Oh, pooh, Crys," Karla offered. "Didn't you ever look at those freshman pictures of mine? I looked just like you. It's just—well, I am three years older. Come on, wear your gray sweater."

"OK, but the first jerk that makes a wisecrack about my being a Lil' Flash is going to get stuffed in his locker with hot oil poured over his head."

"Well, that's quite dainty and ladylike," Mrs. Blake frowned. "Dad had to leave early and said you ought to call up this Mr. Powers and see if he still wants the safe."

"What am I supposed to say?" Crystal asked.

"Well, tell him about how it got in the toolshed, and you think he made a generous offer which you would like to accept," Mrs. Blake suggested.

"How do I know how to reach him? He didn't leave me a phone number," Crystal stalled.

"The sheriff told Dad that he and Mr. Powers were at a meeting last night down in Lewiston, and he mentioned staying at the Riverfront. Give it a try."

Crystal shuffled up the stairs to the phone.

A few minutes later she scooted back down to the kitchen. Karla was helping Mrs. Blake with the breakfast dishes.

She's disgusting, Crystal thought.

"Well, what'd he say?" Mrs. Blake asked.

"He said sure. I think he's genuinely excited about getting the safe. Mom, he said he'd stop by around noon and pick it up. That means we'll be able to buy the stuff at Dartmouth's this afternoon without worrying about the price. Boy, the team is going to be surprised when I tell them."

"Yeah," Karla added, "you'll all be able to dress like Teresa Patterson."

"Teresa . . . oh, I'm so glad that today is the assembly. Then she and Shawn can quit all this secret practicing." Crystal hurried down the stairs to get changed.

She was running out the front door, pulling on her coat, with Karla already in the car when her mother called, "Did you tell Mr. Powers that you opened the safe and it was empty?"

"No, I guess I didn't. But he just wanted it for an antique—I think. Hey, Mom, can we come home for lunch? I'd sort of like to be here when he stops by. Will Dad be back then?"

"He'll be home. Sure you can eat here. I'll fix

some hot soup or something. You really look nice in that sweater," Mrs. Blake added.

"Thanks!" Crystal ran to join Karla.

Some school days dragged at such a pace, Crystal felt that the Lord had made a mistake and made every minute last 120 seconds. This was not one of those days.

The morning blitzed by. Crystal was excited to tell everyone on the rodeo team about the money for new outfits. And because of the adventure with the men the night before, she, Shawn, and Gabrielle were the center of talk all morning (except for a few hints about surprises coming during the assembly).

Karla wanted to stay at school for lunch, so Crystal had to hunt for a ride home. Both Gabrielle and Shawn wanted to come along, but they had to set things up for the assembly.

Crystal wished she had finished her driver's training. She finally caught a ride with Travis Norton, who was also going back to Winchester for lunch.

She had finished eating when a flatbed truck with a hydraulic lift backed up the trail behind the house and stopped near the toolshed. Mr. Powers came to the back door.

Crystal and her dad met him.

"You've got a real business lady there, Mr. Blake," Powers grinned. "She got me to spend a fortune for that old safe. But I'm sure Snake

River Lumber will be happy to have it for historical purposes."

"I can tell you there is one happy rodeo team at Highland High School," Mr. Blake added.

"Here you go, young lady; here's two credit slips. One for the western wear down in Lewiston, and the other for the saddles over in Grangeville." He handed Crystal the papers.

"Wow! This is great, Mr. Powers. Hey, I forgot to tell you, but guess what? Gabrielle and I figured out the combination to the safe and opened it last night. Now you can have the historical display with a safe you can open."

"You what? You opened the safe?" Mr. Powers turned pale.

"Yeah, but it's no big deal. It was empty."

"Empty!" he shouted.

"Boy," Crystal turned to her dad, "I never heard so many people shout over an empty safe."

"It just can't be! It can't be!" Powers kept repeating.

THE NATURAL

MR. POWERS GAPED AT THE EMPTY SAFE IN THE toolshed. Then he walked out into the pine trees next to the house pounding his fist in his hand and muttering.

"I'd say he was disappointed," Mr. Blake whispered to Crystal.

"Does this mean he won't be buying the safe?" Crystal could already imagine having to return to school and tell the team that they didn't get the free outfits after all.

"Well, let's wait and see. I think a deal's a deal, and besides you have the receipts in your hand. I don't know what he's going to do, but I have to go call Mrs. Milton down at Lewis-Clark College. I spent some time with her this morning going over the happenings, and she has a theory. She said if Powers was visibly shaken by seeing an empty safe, I should give her a call. Let me take those receipts in the house. And make sure they haul that thing off. It's nothing but a headache."

Finally, Mr. Powers approached Crystal and the two men he brought with him in the truck.

Gone was his previous generous smile. "Look, kid, you bilked me out of $10,000 for an empty

129

safe. I've got to know if there was anything at all in there when you opened it. Was there anything—any books, letters, documents? Don't give me any bull, I want to know for sure."

"I told Mr. Lavantte all that last night. It was empty. Go ask him." Crystal was defensive.

"Lavantte? He was here? Did he say he was representing the Snake River Lumber Company?"

"Well, not really. . . . Actually he sounded like he was trying to beat you to the safe, but I don't know why."

"Where did he go when he found the safe empty?"

"To the county jail at Nezperce. We don't like folks who make threats. You going over to see him?" Crystal asked.

"Not hardly." He turned to the two men near the truck. "You've got to get me back to Lewiston immediately. I've got to take a plane to Boise as soon as possible."

"What about the safe? You've got to take the safe," Crystal insisted.

"Young lady, I do not have to take anything. If I need it, I'll know where to find it." He jumped in the truck and the dust flew as they hurried off toward the highway.

Crystal's dad appeared at the door. "Hey, they didn't take the safe!"

"They didn't want it. What was so important that they didn't find in the safe?"

"Well, Mrs. Milton, who wrote about the closing of the lumber mill, thinks that Snake River thought there might be incriminating evidence about a premature shutdown of the mill for a tax write-off. Remember I said the workers would get back pay and compensation if that could be proved?"

"Sure, I remember. But if those papers aren't there, then they should be happy. No evidence," Crystal stated.

"Except—maybe they're somewhere else. Maybe the papers and records have been stored while everyone assumed they were destroyed in the fire. If that's true, they could fall into the wrong hands. This means that Powers had better find them first."

"That's why he wanted to get to Boise so fast," Crystal added.

"He's headed to Boise?" Mr. Blake questioned.

"Yeah, that's what he told those guys in the truck," Crystal reported.

Mr. Blake turned to go. "Listen, Crys, there's Travis out front, and I've got to call Mrs. Milton back. She thought maybe Powers was working out of the Portland office. She'll want to know it's Boise. She's going to take a chance at trying to get an injunction against Snake River Lumber Company, barring anyone from their document storage files until the State Attorney General's office can search for those papers."

"You mean folks might still have a chance to

get something out of this?" Crystal asked.

"Well, it's still a long shot. They have to find the books, and then the books have to be clearly incriminating."

Crystal trailed Mr. Blake into the house and called, "I've got to run, Mom. Travis is here."

"Did you finish eating? Here, take an apple at least." Crystal caught the tossed, red apple at the door. "Have fun at the assembly, and hope you have some luck picking out outfits down at Lewiston." Mrs. Blake added, "Do you want your dad to take care of Caleb, or will you be home in time?"

"Uh, if I'm not back by 4:00—oh, I won't make it for sure. I hear Teresa takes forever picking out clothes. You'd better have Dad do it." Crystal ran out the door and jumped into Travis's car.

She could hardly wait to get to school to tell Shawn and Gabrielle about the safe, but discovered they were both still busy. Crystal had momentarily forgotten about the great duet that had taken so much of Shawn's time lately.

As Crystal walked into the Highland High gym and found a seat up front for the show, she felt trapped in a crosscurrent of emotions. Tomorrow was the big rodeo down at Pendleton, and they would be leaving around four in the morning. She was hoping she and Caleb would not let the team down.

At the same time there was the deal with the

safe, and somehow she just didn't think it was all settled. For one thing, what if Dartmouth's wouldn't honor that account that Powers supposedly established? Or what if those men got out of jail and came back around?

Then, she still didn't feel like she had anything cleared up with Shawn. *We need some time to talk . . . just talk,* she thought. *And on top of all that, here's some dumb assembly.*

"If he sings that song to her that he sang to me down in Kamiah, I'm going up on stage and hit him over the head with his guitar," Crystal muttered.

Kids filed in behind her, but she paid little attention. She stared at at the red stage curtain without really seeing it at all.

"How come everybody has to peek out and see the audience?"

Crystal was startled to hear Karla's voice. Her sister sat next to her.

Crystal relaxed a little. "Karla! I didn't see you come in."

"I can see why. You looked lost in space. What happened, did you get rid of the safe?" Karla asked.

"Yes . . . no. Well, actually. See, we got paid, but they didn't want the safe. I mean, they left it and the guy was really burned."

"Shhh! Here it goes. Tell me later." Karla pointed toward the ascending red curtain and the dimming lights.

133

It was really a fun program. Most of the acts were well rehearsed, and most were a satire about life at Highland High. Several seniors did a great pantomime of a freshman's first day at school. Crystal almost cried, she laughed so hard.

Gabrielle came out dressed in a big box and acted like a computerized counselor registering new students. She amazed Crystal with her poise and humor on stage.

Finally, Shawn and Teresa came out. Both wore big silver rodeo buckles. Teresa had on her flashy, tassled, blue silk blouse. Shawn stepped to the mike.

"All right. It's duet time. But we're going to need a little help. As you know, I am one of three new students at Highland High this year. But really, I'm not all that new to you. We've been butting heads with each other at football games and rodeos for years. In fact, half of you are probably related to me. But we do have a couple of girls who are truly outsiders at Highland, and I think it's time we gave them a real north Idaho welcome."

The crowd roared approval, and Karla nudged Crystal, "He's not going to embarrass us, is he?"

"How would I know?" she whispered.

Shawn continued, "Now I would like Karla and Crystal Blake to come up here on the stage with us. Come on, Flash and Lil' Flash, we've got a song for you."

"Crystal, he's your friend. I'll never let you use my blow dryer again," Karla muttered under her breath.

Crystal remembered for the first time since morning that she and Karla were dressed alike. *It's a conspiracy*, she thought. Shawn had the two of them sit on chairs, center stage. He stood on the right side of Crystal, and Teresa on the left side of Karla. Both the girls looked at each other and shrugged, then turned and stared into a sea of dark faces and bright lights.

While still flashing a nervous grin, Crystal spoke between her teeth just loud enough for Shawn to hear. "If you make us do something dumb, you're in big trouble." She never took her eyes off the crowd as she talked.

Shawn just cleared his throat and began playing an introduction on his guitar. Crystal felt her stomach churn and her chest tighten as she watched his every move.

Still strumming the introduction, he stepped to the mike again. "Now, here's a song with words written by Teresa, and the music by none other than Shawn Sorensen. When we get to the chorus, I want you all to join in. The title is, 'You're the Reason God Made California.'"

The audience howled with appreciative laughter. Crystal hated to admit it, but Teresa Patterson could really belt out a song, in a nasal, country sort of way.

"They have the look of big money, those two

blonde beach bunnies," Teresa began. Karla and Crystal blushed and laughed all at the same time. When they got to the chorus the whole school was singing. Crystal realized that they all had printed copies of the words. She was too embarrassed to remember all the words, but it was something about "you can call them Flash and Lil' Flash, but with this you'd better smile. . . . They're one of us now, and goin' to stay awhile. . . . You're the reason God made California. . . ."

There were three verses. One was about Karla. Crystal heard something about the Prairie Heartthrob. *Yeah, that's Karla,* she thought. Then Shawn sang a solo verse about Crystal. "Lil' Flash, the natural . . ." one line went. "The one who reminded us how much fun it is to ride the range."

When the song was over the audience clapped, and Teresa gave Karla a hug. Then Shawn hugged Crystal and kissed her on the cheek. When he did this the whole school went wild with applause.

Crystal felt sweaty all over, and a little dizzy. She didn't know whether to faint or kiss Shawn back. Karla settled the question. She grabbed Crystal's arm and nudged her back down to their seats.

The crowd settled down for the next act. Karla leaned over to Crystal. "Hey, that was quite a song. I think we've been accepted, kid."

136

"Yeah, you said it, Prairie Heartthrob."

"Watch it," Karla warned. "I'll tell Dad you've been kissing boys at school."

"I didn't kiss him, he kissed me," Crystal retorted.

"You bragging or complaining?" Karla poked Crystal in the ribs with her elbow.

After the talent show lots of kids crowded around Crystal and Karla. They laughed and kidded. Shawn walked up carrying his guitar case. Teresa was with him.

"Hey, Teresa," Crystal called above the noise. "You can really sing well."

"Thanks, it was fun. Shawn's a neat guy, you know," Teresa replied.

"Yes . . . I know," Crystal responded. She turned to look at Shawn.

"Hey, sorry to embarrass you up there." He put his guitar case over his shoulder like it was a saddle.

Crystal tried to sound cool. "Don't worry . . . I enjoyed it. A lot of fun. . . ."

"You sure turned red," he laughed.

"I did? Well, sure. Anyway it's no big deal, really."

"It was for me." Shawn wasn't laughing as he looked straight into Crystal's eyes. "I've never kissed anyone before who wasn't related to me."

"Oh, yes, of course, it was a big deal. I mean, it's about the nicest thing that ever happened to me." Crystal couldn't believe that they were

137

talking like this right out in front of a whole crowd of classmates.

"Crystal!" the voice was very deep, but somehow familiar.

She turned to see a tall, strong man in uniform. "Sergeant Kingman! Hi! How's everything down in Kamiah?"

"Slow, since you two left town," he laughed. "You're Shawn, right?"

"Hey, I'm impressed. You remembered our names." Shawn held out his hand.

"It's a small county. Anyway, they sent me up here for you, Crystal. I've got a court order to get you to a phone and give an interview with a judge down in Boise. They wanted me to find you since I'm one of the few on the force that can identify you by sight. Actually, I'm just one of the few on the force." He grinned, "What kind of trouble did you get yourself into this time?"

"Never a dull moment around Crystal," Shawn added. "You ought to see her ride that gray Appy that Kirkland gave her. She's a natural."

"Well, natural, come on to the office; we've got to call Boise." They walked down the hall and turned right toward the administration office.

Sergeant Kingman stopped. "Oh, I need to find Gabrielle Northstar, too."

"She's back in the gym. You can't miss her," Crystal said. "She's the . . ." Suddenly it dawned

on her that Sergeant Kingman was also a Nez
Perce Indian. The words just stuck in Crystal's
throat.

"She's the great-looking, dark-haired one with
the fantastic tan," Shawn finished for her.

"Yeah," Sergeant Kingman acceded, "she's
also my wife's cousin."

Crystal sat next to the telephone as Kingman
dialed a number.

"Sergeant Kingman, Lewis County Sheriff's
Office. Tell Judge Chapman that I've got the
girls here with me. Yes. Yes, sir, they know.
OK." He held his hand over the receiver and
talked to Crystal and Gabrielle.

"This whole conversation is taped. That's
what the little bell in the background means.
When you come on, state your name and address, then just answer the judge's questions."

Sergeant Kingman repeated his name and
rank, testified that he knew both girls by sight,
and that they were the ones about to speak to
the judge.

Crystal talked to the judge for about ten minutes, and Gabrielle only two or three minutes.
When they finished they walked back out into
the hall where Shawn waited. Sergeant Kingman headed back for Kamiah.

"What's that all about?" Shawn questioned.

"Well, I didn't have a chance to tell you, but
Powers showed up for the safe today. He was
really ticked that we opened it up and there was

139

nothing inside. Obviously, he was counting on something being in there."

"I knew it!" Shawn responded.

"Right. So my dad talked to Mrs. Milton, who teaches down at Lewis-Clark, and she thought maybe the Winchester Mill records were stored somewhere else, unknown to even the executives at Snake River Lumber. So she wanted an injunction against the company until a search was made by the State Attorney General's office."

"But why you and Gabrielle?" Shawn asked.

"He needed a witness to testify that the Winchester safe was empty, and someone to state how disappointed Powers was to find it empty," Crystal reported. "I guess the judge isn't too sure there is enough evidence to warrant a search. It's all so circumstantial."

"Anyway, you're all through with that deal, right?" Shawn concluded.

"Yeah, I think so. Except that old safe is still in our toolshed." Crystal went to her locker and chose some books for the weekend.

"Hey, we're supposed to meet Mrs. Patterson, remember?" Gabrielle exclaimed.

Crystal had been right in one thing about Teresa. She was a hard person to please when shopping. It took the boys about five minutes to pick out their shirts. They got two different ones for each member of the team, and they selected new, matching hats. The hats would have to be ordered and steamed before they could get them. Then the boys wandered back into the saddle shop to admire an All Around Cowboy award saddle that was on display.

The girls took at least an hour. They all agreed on one brown print shirt that matched the boys'. But they wanted their second one to be different from the boys', and Teresa insisted that they should get a bright red, silklike shirt with white lace and fringe.

Crystal objected. "Red is definitely not my color," she insisted. "My shade of blonde hair does not complement red."

Finally the girls appealed to Mrs. Patterson. "Well," she said, "red does look nice on some of you, especially Gabrielle with that jet black hair. She would certainly be the star of the team."

Instantly, Teresa decided that the blue shirts that Crystal preferred would be just fine.

To their amazement, Power's credit was really good. He kept his word.

It was dark by the time Crystal got back up the mountain to Winchester. She carted her purchases into the house and went outside to double-check on Caleb.

"OK, big guy, tomorrow we will show them. I mean, you will show them, and I'll come along for the ride. Get lots of rest. You've got a long haul tomorrow." She didn't linger in the frosty outdoors.

Crystal did not need anyone to tell her to get to bed early. She knew that the 4:00 a.m. departure would be tough enough even when rested. She laid out the clothes she wanted to wear and packed a duffel with some spare things. She polished her boots and took time for some Bible reading. Shawn called while she was brushing her teeth. She took the call in the office.

"Listen, I've got to talk to you," he said. "About the song and all."

"And all?" She sat the phone on the floor and flopped down next to it.

"Yeah, the kiss . . . you know. I'm sorry about that."

"You are?"

"Well, I've really been thinking about it."

"You have?"

"Yeah."

"Me, too," Crystal was glad that he couldn't see her blush.

"Well, I really believe that I shouldn't have done it."

"Oh, yeah?"

"What I mean is, I should have asked you if it would be all right." He sounded apologetic.

"Oh . . . yeah . . . well. But that's OK. It really did fit the situation, I thought."

"That's the way I felt, too, at the time. Anyway I was . . . I was . . . I was praying and I felt real strong that I should call. So, next time I'm going to kiss you I promise I'll ask first. OK?"

"Oh . . . sure. Yeah." Crystal realized she was mumbling.

"Well, see you early in the morning, and I do mean early." And he hung up.

Crystal sat, dreaming, on the floor for a moment, then waltzed to her bed with one thought in mind. *Next time . . . he said "next time."*

RODEO GIRL

CRYSTAL HAD HARDLY SETTLED INTO BED WHEN she heard the phone ring. For a moment she thought that it might be Shawn calling. "To say, 'Please disregard previous conversation,'" she laughed to herself.

A few minutes later her dad came into her room, "You awake, princess?"

"Sure. What's up?"

He sat on the edge of her bed. "That was a call from Mrs. Milton, the professor who's pushing through this thing with the safe. It seems like the judge did grant an injunction against Snake River Lumber Company. He gave the Attorney General's office twenty-four hours to search the company's documents. I guess they sent a team over there and ransacked the place, but they haven't found a thing yet. Mrs. Milton is driving down to Boise right now to help in the search. If nothing is found by 2:00 p.m. tomorrow, the case will be dropped."

"Maybe we've been wrong," Crystal suggested. "I mean, it was only a theory."

"Well, I certainly hope we are right," Mr. Blake sighed, "because Snake River Lumber is so upset at this injunction that they filed suit against the State of Idaho, Mrs. Milton, and one Crystal LuAnne Blake."

"What?" Crystal sat straight up in bed.

"You are being sued by one of the biggest corporations in the northwest."

"What did I do?"

"Defamation of character, they say."

"What does it mean?" She sounded frantic.

"Well, if the state finds some incriminating evidence, Snake River will drop the charges. If not, you go to trial. But don't worry. They would have to convince a jury that you deliberately set out to hurt the company."

"But I didn't!" Crystal pleaded.

"I know that. Don't worry; they're just trying to save face," he concluded. "Let's leave that with the Lord."

Crystal tried to listen as her dad prayed, but she kept getting a panicky feeling about the suit. Mr. Blake started to leave when Crystal sat back up in bed again. "Dad. Did they tell you how much in damages they were suing for?"

"Hey, what's a half million dollars to a rodeo girl like you? You can earn it in, say, 300 years," he laughed. "Now get some sleep."

Crystal lay there staring at the ceiling in the darkness of her bedroom. *Get some sleep? Half a million dollars. Sweet dreams, rodeo girl.* She turned over on her stomach, scrunched the pillow under her head, let out a big sigh, and tried to sort her tumble of thoughts.

"There is no human way that anyone can get up this early in the morning," Crystal moaned as she buzzed out of the shower and back into her room. "It's pitch dark and freezing out there!" She thought about Karla and Allyson, both of whom were sound asleep. She tried to think about the great time she would have at the rodeo, but all she could think about was six hours of driving across Washington and down into Oregon.

When Crystal emerged from her room, her dad was out loading Caleb in a big school trailer. Her mom was cooking breakfast. Crystal, Shawn, Gabrielle, and Travis would use this trailer, and Crystal's dad would pull it behind the Blakes' pickup.

The school's trailers and assorted pickups motored through the mountains long before daylight. Crystal, Shawn, and Gabrielle sat in the back of the pickup covered by a camper shell. Travis, prone to car sickness, rode up front with Mr. Blake. The sliding glass window between the cab and the camper shell was open in order to let the heater push some air to the back.

During the first several hours all three dozed off. Just before they got to Walla Walla the caravan pulled over, and everyone piled out to walk the horses. It was cold, but it was clear. The fresh air helped to wake up Crystal.

"Did I tell you about being sued?" Crystal addressed Shawn and Gabrielle as they led their horses back toward the trailer.

"Sued? For what?" Gabrielle shook her head. She couldn't believe what she was hearing.

"Defamation of character of the Snake River Lumber Company. Really, if the state doesn't find any evidence down in Boise, the company is going to sue me for one-half million dollars!" Crystal stopped and looked at Shawn and then Gabrielle.

"Wow, there goes your piggy bank," Shawn laughed.

"It's so absurd. Why are they doing this to me?"

"Nice folks," Shawn added. "Why didn't they sue me and Gabrielle as well?"

"You didn't testify to the judge," Crystal remarked.

"I did. But of course they can't sue me. I was on the reservation land. Reservation law, you know. Besides, they knew they couldn't get much from an Indian."

"Maybe your folks could temporarily adopt me," Crystal laughed.

"Sorry, paleface. You're on your own," Gabrielle replied.

At 12:30 they pulled into the grass-covered parking lot next to Pendleton's high school rodeo grounds. Everyone cried for food. While a couple of the parents headed for a supply of hamburgers and soft drinks, the team got their horses out and ready.

This was Crystal's tenth time to compete since getting Caleb at the end of August. Most of the time it had been little after-school rodeos around the Camas Prairie. Pendleton was different.

Kids in Pendleton, Oregon, anticipated the day when they would win some silver at the annual Pendleton Roundup—one of the greatest rodeos in North America. And the Pendleton High School rodeo team was one of the best in the country. Crystal anticipated tough competition.

Caleb pranced in a seeming good mood. Crystal was beginning to understand that horses were a lot like people. Some days were good, and some days were bad. There didn't seem to be a lot of logic in Caleb's condition. The only time Crystal could count on him always being alert and aggressive was cutting out cattle. Some hidden urge always gripped him and he performed with determination.

Crystal rode him around the trailers, across the parking lot, and into an adjoining field. She trotted him for a while. It was always the same. Give her Caleb, a clear day, and space to ride. There was nothing better in the whole world. She didn't know if the others could feel what she did. *Maybe they have been riding for so long that it doesn't phase them anymore. I hope that never happens to me.*

Every person ought to find a place where they

are able to really be at home and like themselves. No pretense, no games, no putting out just for someone else. This is my place. Lord, thanks. I'm ready to ride!

"Hey, Gabrielle," Crystal shouted, "are we going to win or what!"

"Listen, Lil' Flash, if we don't, we will scare them to death anyway. I think we could make it close."

Crystal's three events happened to be the last three of the day, so that meant a long wait before she rode. She sat on the rail of the fence with Gabrielle and watched as the rodeo started with saddle bronc riding. Highland riders did a good job, but two of the guys from Pendleton outshone them. "Wow," Crystal pointed out to the arena, "look at that one guy ride."

"Yeah, that's Dan Stonewell. He's always at the All-Indian Rodeo over in Joseph. Good, huh?" Gabrielle nodded.

"Do you know everyone in every rodeo?" Crystal laughed.

"Only the good-looking ones with natural tans," she kidded.

Highland could only get a third and a fifth in the saddle bronc rides. Bull riding was not much better—Pendleton finished first, second, third in bull riding.

The first sign of life in the Highland team came in the goat roping. Highland led after the first round, but that only seemed to spur on the

Pendleton team. They excelled in the second round, but Highland finished second and fifth.

Team roping reversed the trend. Shawn and Travis got off to a fast start. Shawn, acting as heeler, had a stunning throw. Even Pendleton team gave him applause. When the event ended, Highland finished first, second, and fourth. Crystal felt there was a sign of hope.

That hope magnified in breakaway roping. It was Gabrielle's turn to shine. She was equaled by a red-haired girl from Pendleton who rode a stunning white horse. The event ended in a tie for first. Highland also held second place.

Crystal figured that bareback riding would go much the same way as the other riding events, with Pendleton coming out on top. She, and many others, were surprised when Chet Nickles, another freshman at Highland, put on the gutsiest ride of the day on a big black bull named Sunfish. Chet finished second, and everyone gathered to congratulate him. He was, however, the only Highland team member to pick up points.

Crystal leaned over to Gabrielle. "It doesn't look too good, does it?"

"Hey, we haven't gotten to our strongest events. Hang on. We'll do it," Gabrielle encouraged.

Steer wrestling came next. Shawn came over to Crystal, "Hey, Lil' Flash, come on. I want you to haze."

"You're serious?"

"Come on, partner, you can do it." He motioned to her.

"I swear, that guy has the greatest eyes," Gabrielle swooned.

"Oh, go rope a goat," Crystal hit Gabrielle with her hat.

"Brett Murray is the one to beat," Shawn said as they waited their turn. If I can get by him, it will go."

Most of the times were between 12.5 and 14 seconds. Brett turned in a 10.3, well into first place.

"Wow, that's fast." Crystal shook her head.

"Piece of cake, kiddo. Come on, it's our turn."

They entered the arena, and Shawn headed behind the barrier. Crystal felt very unsure of her role, but Caleb acted as though he knew the game well. All of a sudden the flag fell and one scared calf tore out of the chute, with Caleb and Crystal on his right side. In what seemed to Crystal no time at all, Shawn was down on the animal and had him thrown.

The announcer stated Shawn's time as 9.32.

"I'm impressed," Crystal exploded.

"I've had a lot better. Brett is going to go all out next time. I'll be going out before him, so I've got to have such a great time that he's psyched out. Give Caleb a big kick right at first and jump that calf right back at me, OK? I'm going to try to fly right off of there."

151

The next round exhibited an obvious contest between Shawn and Brett. Shawn rode his horse back into the box and gave Crystal a thumbs-up sign. She nodded back at him. The calf started to bolt out of the gate and Crystal kicked Caleb hard with her heels. He jumped out so fast it was all Crystal could do to hold on. She managed to fudge him to the left, and then Shawn was alongside diving on the calf and throwing him to the ground. The audience roared.

Then, there was a long pause. Finally, the announcer broke the silence. "This one is for real. Shawn Sorensen, for Highland, just had a time of 5.7. Boy, that is one quick time."

Brett seemed demoralized. He had a respectable 11.1 for an easy second place.

The only event left before Crystal's was calf roping. She thought that this would be Shawn's strongest event. It turned out that Brett was not one to settle with second place. His first time out, he beat Shawn by two full seconds. The second go-around found Shawn chasing a black-and-white calf that would cut back and forth. Shawn roped him quickly, but not quite quick enough. He had to settle for a second place.

"How does it look now?" Crystal asked Gabrielle.

"We just don't have the depth. We've got someone in the thick of things in every event, but Pendleton keeps picking up points on down the line. We're probably out of it."

"Hey, we've got a chance," Teresa climbed up beside them. All we need is the first three places in each of the next three events."

"We could actually win?"

"Well, tie at least," Teresa reported.

The cutting horse event was next. Shawn issued Crystal last-minute instructions, as though she had not been sitting there watching the whole rodeo.

"You've got two chances. The second round will reverse the order of the first. They're using two judges, so you will have a possibility of 160 points each go-around. Remember, let Caleb take charge, and you just keep him hustling. If you try to guide him, they'll penalize you."

Crystal was the first one to work on the herd. Caleb tore into the cattle, singled out a white-faced Hereford and pushed him bawling and screaming right out into the center of the arena. She could faintly hear the crowd cheer. They had done it. She had withstood the pressure and done it.

"All right!" Gabrielle yelled.

Crystal's score was 150.

Shawn came over to congratulate her. "Hey, cowgirl, nice ride."

"Thanks, partner," she beamed. Crystal stayed close to the outside gate of the arena to watch the others. At the end of the round, Crystal led by seven points. Having been first in the first go-around, she was now last. By the time it was her turn again, her closest competitor was her teammate, Dusty.

"Hey, you only need a 135 to take it all. Come on, you can do it," Gabrielle called.

Once again Crystal rode the big gray Appaloosa out into the center of the arena, and once again Caleb took charge. *Never, never is he this happy*, Crystal thought.

This time the animal that was singled out was solid black, but the results were the same. And Caleb was just getting warmed up. Crystal had to fight him after the event was over from returning for another animal on his own.

The announcer came on. "Folks, you don't have to be an expert to know who won our cutting event. It wasn't even close. Crystal Blake of Highland finished with an incredible 154, making a 304 total. You won't see that every day. Great job, Crystal."

It took awhile for it to sink in. Crystal was not used to winning things. She had always been in second place. It was a nice, safe place to be. Nobody ever tried to dethrone the runner-up. In fact no one even remembered your name. Suddenly, the impact hit her. Not third, not second, but first place. She was not just fair, nor was she merely good, she was the best of the show.

It felt funny to her. She wanted just to slip into the crowd and think it all through. But her teammates were busy congratulating her.

Pole bending came next. It was not her event,

but it was one that she was entered in. Fortunately it *was* Teresa's event. As Crystal pushed Caleb through the course she always felt as if he thought all this running around poles was a silly game. Crystal's 25.6 did not place her in contention. Gabrielle had a 21.9 and was in fourth place. Teresa had the best ride of the team with a 20.8.

Unfortunately it was not the best in Pendleton. The second go-around didn't change the standings, and Teresa, having her best day ever, still finished second. Crystal figured that Teresa would really be depressed. As in every event, Gabrielle finished in the top five.

"You okay?" Crystal asked Teresa.

"Hey, sure, no big. I'll ride against them another day. It's not my first rodeo." Teresa sounded cocky.

As Crystal turned to go back to the arena, Teresa called, "Lil' Flash! Listen, thanks for asking."

It was the last event of the day, barrel racing, and the match was technically over. Teresa counseled Crystal and Gabrielle. "Let's try to take three out of five places. I want us to go out shining." Teresa had a determination in her eyes that Crystal recognized as the look of a winner.

Both Teresa and Gabrielle flew through the barrel pattern in perfect style and form. Teresa had a 16.3 and Gabrielle a 16.1. Crystal entered the arena for her turn. Her concentration was

155

broken when the announcer called for Mr. Matthew Blake to take a phone call. She pushed the thought from her mind and patted Caleb. "All right, champ, show them just how good you really are." Then Crystal quickly spurred him on.

Caleb dashed off with a sudden burst of speed, made a good cut around the first barrel, raced to the second and made another quick cut. Crystal couldn't keep him up against the barrel on the third cut and then raced him home.

Her time was 19.4. "Respectable, but not a winner," she told herself. "That's the real Crystal. Respectable, but not a winner."

During the second round, the contest between Gabrielle and Teresa intensified with Gabrielle's ride of 16.0. Teresa would need a 15.8 to tie and an incredible 15.7 to win. There was no talking to Teresa. Her concentration was so intense people actually stepped back away from her. She strutted on her beautiful horse and inhaled deep breaths while Crystal and Gabrielle watched from the fence. They stared in amazement as she pushed her horse through three short, quick turns and whipped him on across the finish line. Teresa jumped off her horse and led him over to the judges' stand.

"Fifteen point six," the announcer stated.

Gabrielle was the first off the rail to congratulate Teresa. Crystal was right behind. "Teresa! One great ride!"

"Yeah, thanks." She smiled and started to look a bit relaxed.

"That was the best ride I ever saw," Gabrielle added.

"No kidding? You mean that?" Teresa gave Gabrielle a hug.

"Lil' Flash—you're up," Shawn called.

Crystal had almost forgotten her final round. She mounted Caleb and rode him inside the gate. "Well, big guy, did you see how Teresa did that? You ready to show them? Heyaa! Go!"

Caleb tore around the first barrel so fast Crystal felt lucky just to hang on, the second turn spun also, and the third seemed to be the shortest cut Caleb had ever made. She pushed him on down the line, and he was flying as he crossed the finish line.

The announcement came: "17.7."

Crystal laughed at Gabrielle, "17.7? I thought I was going a hundred miles an hour. How do you guys do it?"

"Lil' Flash," Teresa called, "you did it! Fifth place in the barrels. Nice riding."

"Really? Fifth place? All right!"

The events were over. The judges verified all the scores to announce the team winner and the All Around Cowboy and All Around Cowgirl. Crystal's dad met her at the trailer. "Great riding, princess."

She reached up and gave him a big hug. "Thanks. It was fun. Did you see Teresa's ride?

She's a tornado out there."

"That's what I heard. I missed it," he added. "Had a phone call from Mom."

"Mom?"

"Yes, she wanted us to know that Mrs. Milton called. Guess what? They found the documents from the Winchester Mill down in a storage room in Boise. She thinks the evidence will get some settlement for both the town and the workers."

"No fooling, they found it? Where?"

"Well, it wasn't in any of the files, but someone thought to look in an old desk that had a lot of boxes piled on it. It turned out someone decided that it would be a shame to burn the desk up with the Winchester Mill, and they had shoved all the corporate papers from that safe in a desk drawer. They've been sitting there for twenty-five years." He smiled.

"No more lawsuit?" Crystal took off her hat and brushed back her hair.

"You got it."

"Hey, come on, Crys," Shawn hollered. "They are announcing the final score."

"Well, folks, you saw some great rodeo today. Pendleton High School has defeated Highland High and remains undefeated. But I don't want those Highland High cowboys and cowgirls to be disappointed. That was the closest rodeo Pendleton has had all year. And not only that, the All Around Cowboy award goes to Shawn

Sorensen of Highland High, and the All Around Cowgirl award to Gabrielle Northstar of Highland. These two racked up the most individual points of the day on either team. Nice going, Shawn and Gabrielle."

Shawn and Gabrielle went up to the judges' stand to get their belt buckles while Crystal leaned against the fence and waited.

"Hi, I'm Brett Murray. You've got one great cutting horse."

Crystal turned to see the boy from Pendleton standing next to her. "Thanks . . . his name is Caleb."

"What's your name?" he pressed.

"Oh, I'm Crystal." *He does have a nice smile,* she thought.

"Well, I was wondering if you would like . . ."

"The answer is no, she wouldn't."

Crystal twirled around to see Shawn walking up beside her. He continued, "Murray, you aren't trying to cut in on my girl, are you?"

"Your girl? She's your girl?" Brett stammered.

"You got it. Right, Crystal?" Shawn slipped his arm around her waist.

She smiled and slipped her arm around Shawn.

"You really Shawn's girl?" Brett looked right at Crystal.

"Yup," she said, and the two walked arm in arm out of the arena.

For adventure, excitement, and even romance . . .
Read these Quick Fox books

CRYSTAL Books by Stephen and Janet Bly

How many fourteen-year-old girls have been chased by the cavalry, stopped a stagecoach, tried rodeo riding, and discovered buried treasure? Crystal Blake has. You never know what new adventure Crystal will find in the next chapter!

1 Crystal's Perilous Ride
2 Crystal's Solid Gold Discovery
3 Crystal's Rodeo Debut
4 Crystal's Mill Town Mystery
5 Crystal's Blizzard Trek
6 Crystal's Grand Entry

MARCIA Books by Norma Jean Lutz

Marcia Stallings has every girl's dream—her own horse! And she intends to pursue her dream of following her mother's footsteps into the show arena—no matter what the obstacles.

1 Good-bye, Beedee
2 Once Over Lightly